jail break

Cranshaw jerked his Colt free and continued forward at a crouch. The horses were pulling away from him, and he dropped to one knee to fire a shot over the heads of the riders.

One turned, and Lex knew it was Barton Rawlings.

Rawlings jerked the reins and wheeled his mount in a circle so tight it nearly stumbled. Charging back toward Lex, he aimed a pistol and squeezed the trigger. The bullet slammed into the shake shingles just over his head and Lex hit the deck. There was no cover anywhere.

Rawlings was grinning from ear to ear, his teeth glittering in the sunlight, his mustache wriggling as his face contorted into a parody of amusement. He fired again, and the bullet passed through the brim of Lex's hat before burying itself in the wall behind him.

Also by
Dan Mason

THE RANGER
BORDER BANDITS
COMANCHE RAIDERS
RANGE WAR
TRACK DOWN
APACHE THUNDER
NUECES STRIP

**Published by
HarperPaperbacks**

ATTENTION: ORGANIZATIONS AND CORPORATIONS

Most HarperPaperbacks are available at special quantity
discounts for bulk purchases for sales promotions, premiums,
or fund-raising. For information, please call or write:
Special Markets Department, HarperCollins Publishers,
10 East 53rd Street, New York, N.Y. 10022.
Telephone: (212) 207-7528. Fax: (212) 207-7222.

DAN MASON

THE RANGER

THE END OF THE LINE

HarperPaperbacks
A Division of HarperCollinsPublishers

This is a work of fiction. The characters, incidents, and dialogues are products of the author's imagination and are not to be construed as real. Any resemblance to actual events or persons, living or dead, is entirely coincidental.

HarperPaperbacks *A Division of* HarperCollins*Publishers*
10 East 53rd Street, New York, N.Y. 10022

Cover illustration by Larry Schwinger

First printing: June 1993

Printed in the United States of America

HarperPaperbacks and colophon are trademarks of HarperCollins*Publishers*

10 9 8 7 6 5 4 3 2 1

THE END
OF THE LINE

MONROE WAS about as hot and dusty a town as Lex Cranshaw had ever seen. It was the kind of place where people didn't so much settle as stop rolling when the wind let up. They collected like leaves against a fence. But Lex was tired and hungry, and as thirsty as he could ever remember being. And Monroe, according to all the prognosticators, had a future, because the railroad was coming. The Texas and Western was slowly snaking its way westward and Monroe just happened to be in the way.

As he rode down the main street, small clouds of dust ballooned out from the hooves of his big roan stallion, drifted a few feet, then, exhausted, collapsed to wait for the next hoof, the next boot, the next gust of hot wind to give them a push. Even the buildings, their boards not so much weathered as bleached by the hot sun, and made brittle by the dusty wind, seemed on the verge of heat prostration.

People had been pouring into Texas for thirty years, ever since the end of the Mexican War, drawn by tales of limitless space, fortunes to be made with a little luck and a lot of sweat, and the convenient memory that allowed a man to reweave the fabric of his own history in a way that was more suitable to his new neighbors, no questions asked. But if Lex had to guess, for Monroe, railroad or not, prosperity was not in the cards. He could see that.

The few ranches he'd passed on the road from Higginbotham looked as if they were just hanging on by tooth and claw. The cattle were gaunt, there wasn't much grass, and what there was looked like straw. He'd been all over the state, and if there was a place with a bleaker prospect, he had yet to see it. But stranger things had happened.

And since beggars can't be choosers, a hot meal and real feathers under his weary bones would be welcome, at least for a night. The rumor was the man he had been hunting was out there to the east somewhere, working for the T and W. He would head out the next morning once more dragging himself into the hot, bleak spaces that seemed so overwhelming, that with all its dreary comforts, Monroe was welcome. A battered sign identified a saloon as The Wet Whistle, and that was as good an invitation as he needed. He nodded at a handful of cowboys lounging in front of the saloon, their chairs tilted back against the wall. One of them tossed him a casual salute as he dismounted, tied the roan off, then clapped four days of trail dust from his clothes.

"Look a mite dry, cowboy," the one who'd saluted cackled. "Might be almost human, though, you clap a little more dust from your jeans."

"I haven't been this thirsty since hell froze over,"

Lex said. He kicked his boots against the boardwalk before climbing onto it, then pushed on inside.

The place was hot, and stank of stale beer and damp sawdust. He shambled to the bar, his spurs clinking with each hollow thud of a boot heel on the thick, wooden planking of the floor. Another half-dozen cowhands lined the bar in pairs. They were talking quietly, and paid him no mind.

The bartender, a man with arms like hams and a barrel chest that seemed too large for his head, sidled toward him, a damp towel swiping at the bar as he moved along. "What'll it be, cowboy?" he asked. He scratched his thick red beard while he waited, then smoothed the shaggy ginger eyebrows that seemed ready to overwhelm the watery blue eyes beneath them.

"Beer'll be fine," Lex said. "And a shot of rye, if you have it."

The bartender laughed. "This ain't a church, part-ner. You bet I got rye." He moved to the tap, drew a beer in a mug that must have been transparent at one time in the distant past, and slid it along the bar, the passage lubricated by the mug's overflow. Snatching a shot glass made of the same murky crystal from a damp towel on the mantel behind the bar, he tilted a bottle of rye until the pale amber neared the brim, clapped the whiskey down in its place and reached back without looking to set the shot glass on the bar.

The bartender wiped his hands on his bar rag, then leaned against the mantel, his massive arms folded across his thick trunk. "Passing through?" he asked.

Lex nodded. "Yep. That I am."

"Reason I ask, it's been a while since we had any new blood in town. Seems like we don't catch many a fancy here in Monroe. Like maybe folks got better places to go, even if they got *no* place to go, if you know what I mean."

"Why's that?"

The bartender shrugged. "Who the hell knows? Who knows why one town sticks and another one don't. Ain't no reason for none of it, I reckon. Just the luck of the draw. And Monroe's about run out of luck. Not that it ever had much to begin with, far as I can tell. I been here near nine years now, and . . . course, the railroad'll change all that. Or so they tell me. I got no place to go, so I reckon I can hang on and see if they're right."

"Marty, why'nt you quit your jabberin' and let the man have his drink? You been runnin' that same story past ever' pair of new ears stumbled in here as long as I've known you." The speaker was one of the hands down the bar. Lex nodded to him, tilted the shot glass back and drained the rye. Its heat felt good going down, cutting through the dust and making him feel, if not alive, then a little further from death's door than when he rode in.

The cowboy moved down the bar a couple of paces, just close enough to extend a hand. Lex shook it, and the man said, "Name's Roy Childress. Don't pay no attention to Marty, here. He's got that song and dance down to an art, but he's a one trick pony. Ever' once in a while I threaten to take my business somewhere's else, but since there's only three sa-loons in town, and the other two're even worse than this, he knows I ain't going nowhere."

Lex smiled. "I've seen worse," he said.

"Just don't remember where or when, right?"

Lex laughed. "Can't knock the man's rye, anyhow."

Marty pushed away from the mantel and propped his hamlike forearms on the bar. "See that, Roy. What've I been tellin' you?"

"Lies, mostly," Childress said, grinning at the bartender. "And quite a few, at that."

Lex took a sip of his beer.

Childress yanked a stool closer and sat down. "Looking for work, are you?"

Lex shook his head. "Nope. Just passing through."

"Got a job, then?"

Lex nodded. "That I do."

"Sounds like you might be one of two things," Childress said.

"What might those be?" Lex asked.

"An outlaw or a lawman."

"I'm no outlaw," Lex said, grinning.

Childress nodded. "What then, a marshal?"

"Texas Ranger."

"You're joking! What in hell brings you all the way out here in the middle of nowhere? Ain't been no rustling. Nobody wants them scrawny cows. We don't get some rain soon, they'll likely dry up altogether and head west on the first stiff breeze. And there ain't enough money in the damn bank to make it worth anybody's while to try and hold it up."

"I'm looking for someone."

"A fugitive, huh?"

Lex nodded. He didn't really like the idea of talking too much about his reasons for being in Monroe. It seemed like there was little enough to get excited about. That meant lots of idle talk, and the less of that the better. If Barton Rawlings were where he was rumored to be, it wouldn't take much for him to get wind of Lex. But now that Childress had gotten his hooks into some juicy gossip, it didn't look much like he was about to let it go.

"Man wanted for murder. That's about all I'm at liberty to discuss," Lex said.

"Well, hell, man, maybe we can give you a hand. I know just about everybody in these parts. Ain't been nobody new in four or five years, except for them railroad boys over east of here." Childress stopped suddenly, as if he'd just seen the light. "That's it, ain't it? You're lookin' for one of them roughnecks workin' on the Texas and Western. Most of 'em been in here one time or another. That's it, ain't it?"

Lex nodded. "That's it. But I'd appreciate it if you'd keep that to yourself. The last thing I need is for him to cut and run. It's taken me a week to get here, and I don't fancy another week back home, empty-handed."

"Well, hell, you bring him in, and we can handle the rest. There's lots of rope in Monroe, for sure, and not a whole hell of a lot to do with it."

Lex shook his head. "Thanks, but no thanks, Mister Childress. That isn't how it's done. I got to bring him to Austin, for trial."

"Waste of good money, you ask me. If he done it, and I don't guess you'd be chasin' across a hellacious place like this if he didn't, seems like short and sweet is the best way to handle it."

Lex sipped some more of his beer, licked the foam from his lips, and said, "I got to talk to your sheriff. You'll have to excuse me."

Childress nodded as if he understood, something Lex was far from convinced was actually the case.

Downing the rest of his beer, Lex started for the door. Before he reached it, he heard the sound of gunshots. Pulling his Colt, he dashed out onto the boardwalk, conscious of the rush of feet behind him on the floor.

The lounging cowhands were on their feet, staring down the street toward the eastern end of town. "The hell's going on?" one of them said. He glanced over his shoulder at Lex as if he expected the Ranger to have an answer.

Childress slipped in behind Lex. "Looks like you brung a little excitement with you after all," he said, clapping Lex on the shoulder.

Two men on horseback were just breaking over a hill and heading into the town. Two more gunshots cracked, their echoes slapping the walls of the town and sounding feeble and distant. The spurts of gunsmoke went straight up, and Lex knew the men were firing to get attention.

He ran into the street, then turned to Childress. "You'd better run and get the sheriff," he said.

Childress nodded, and sprinted down the boardwalk toward the west end of the street. Lex raced up the center of the town, his boots chuffing as they slapped the inch-deep powder in the street. The two riders, apparently thinking he was the law, yelled something, but they were too far away for him to catch the words.

As they closed on him, they reined in, skidding to a halt so abruptly that one of the men was nearly thrown from the saddle. Lex could tell by their clothes they were not cowhands, and judging by the way they sat their mounts, he assumed horseback was not their usual means of transportation.

"What's all the fuss, gents?" Lex asked.

"Been a terrible row at the Texas and Western work camp," one of the men shouted as he struggled to get his feet out of the stirrups. "You the sheriff?"

Lex shook his head. "He's been sent for. You want to tell me what's up?"

The man shook his head. "Got to talk to the sheriff. Mister Crandall said . . ."

"Who's Mister Crandall?"

"The T and W man. He come by to see how we was doing, and . . ."

"Two men dead," the other man said. "Maybe more. It was really ugly. Guns and I don't know what all . . ."

Lex heard someone approaching behind him and turned to see Roy Childress trailing in the wake of a wiry little man with gray hair and a drooping mustache that was as much salt as pepper.

Brushing past Lex, the sheriff said, "I'll handle this, son, if you don't mind."

THE SHERIFF, Lute Olson, grabbed one of the two railroaders by the arm and started to drag him toward the boardwalk. "Come on, damn it, man," Olson barked. "This ain't no place to be talkin' about such things."

Olson looked at Lex then, and said, "You want to help, mister, you grab that other sorry excuse for a man and bring him along. We'll go to my office and see if we can get a few straight answers out of 'em before we go off on some wild-goose chase."

The two pairs, lawman and railroad man, thumped along the boardwalk, with the restless and bored cowhands milling along in their wake, like wild cats following a fishmonger's wagon. When they reached the sheriff's office, Olson shoved his companion inside, then held the door open for Lex and his man. Inside, Olson slammed the door, then opened it a crack to peer outside for a moment. "You men run along to the saloon. There ain't nothin' for you to do here. Go on, now, git!" And he slammed

9

the door, leaving the wranglers mumbling in the street.

Only then did Olson stick out a hand to Lex. "Lute Olson," he said. "Who're you?"

"Name's Cranshaw. Lex Cranshaw."

"Somebody said you was a Ranger. That right?"

Lex nodded. "That's right."

"What brings you to hell's vestibule, Mister Cranshaw? I know you ain't here for the scenery."

"Looking for a man named Barton Rawlings. Wanted for murder. The last word we had, he was working for the Texas and Western, probably at the head of the line."

"Can't say I ever heard of the gent. You know what he looks like?"

Before Lex could answer, one of the two winded railroad men said, "I sure as hell do. He was one of them what done the shooting."

Olson tilted his head back as if he were trying to balance something on his widow's peak. "That a fact?" he asked. "And who might you be? Maybe we should get first things first."

The man nodded, looked at his partner, then looked at a rickety chair in the corner. "Mind if I sit down, Sheriff?"

"Suit yourself."

The man walked to the chair as if his legs were made of India rubber, lowered himself gingerly while keeping one hand braced on the chair's rather frail-looking ladder back. His companion scratched his bony chest through his dusty denim shirt, then took a seat on the front edge of Olson's cluttered desk.

The man in the chair said, "My name's John Kinkaid. I been working for Texas and Western since sixty-seven. Come out here from Pennsylvania, right after the war. When they started . . ."

"Mister Kinkaid," Olson said, "I ain't interested in your autobiography, unless it has somethin' to do with the shooting that brought you all the way here this morning. Does it?"

Kinkaid shook his head. "No, sir, it don't."

"Fine, then why don't you just cut right to the bone, and tell me what happened. Before you do, though, you mind tellin' me who this is?" Olson cocked a thumb at the second railroader, who cleared his throat and introduced himself. "Peter Shillig, Sheriff. I work for . . ."

"I know, I know. You worked for T and W, ever since Jesus was a pup. But that ain't what I want to hear, now is it, Mister Shillig?"

Shillig shook his head. "No, I suppose not."

"Good, you just go right on supposin' while Mister Kinkaid tells me what I want to know, all right?"

Shillig grunted, ran a hand through the tangled straw that passed for his hair, then scraped a callused hand under his lantern jaw. "Sure, sure."

Kinkaid leaned forward, his round face glowing a deep pink color, whether from sunburn or the exertion of his ride, Lex couldn't tell. Olson nodded his head, and it was like priming a pump. Kinkaid bobbed his head, his eyelids fluttered, and he started to talk, the words beginning slowly, then gushing out in a torrent.

"The payroll was late. Seems like it's late a lot, since the scandal, you know. Credit Mobilier. Hard to raise money, and I don't know if Mister Scott, that's

Thomas Scott, who owns the T and W, can get enough to finish the job. Anyhow, like I said, the payroll was late, and the men were getting kind of jittery. They ain't been paid in more than three months, and the last time they were shorted a month, and so they don't particularly want to wait around but they know if they don't, then they never will get what's comin' to them, most likely anyway, and . . ."

Olson held up a hand. "Whoa, hold on, hold on, there, Johnny . . . wait just a minute. You said there was a shootin', and I suppose it was that what brung you here, not the money troubles of your Mister Scott. That right?"

Kinkaid bobbed his head again, and Lex was reminded of an apple in a galvanized tub. "That's right, that's exactly right, Sheriff. There was a shootin'."

"Then, if it ain't too much trouble, would you mind telling me about it? Keep it simple. I'm just a dumb sheriff in a backwater town that might not even be here the next time a strong wind blows through."

"Like I said, the men were in a foul mood. I'm the construction foreman, and Mister Shillig is the accountant and paymaster, so naturally, they made their complaints known to us. I tried to explain that the payroll was delayed, that's all. It's coming from New Orleans, and I expect it in a day or two or three. But that wasn't good enough. The next thing I know, they were all grumbling and cursing. They went looking for Henry Schuster, and . . ."

"Who's he?" Olson demanded.

"He's the project engineer. I guess you could say he's the boss, the man in charge, anyhow, and . . ."

"And what did Mister Schuster tell the men?"

"The same thing I tried to tell them. But they were in no mood to listen. Then one of them, the one Mister Cranshaw asked about, Rawlings, started to get ugly. He grabbed Mister Schuster and threatened to beat him to death if he didn't get his pay. That seemed to shock some of the men, and they backed off a little, but Rawlings didn't stop. When Mister Schuster said there was nothing he could do until the pay train arrived, Rawlings said maybe he would just take his back pay out of Mister Schuster's hide."

Kinkaid stopped to swallow, and in the abrupt silence, the gulp echoed off the high ceiling.

"Go on, Johnny," Olson prompted. "What happened next?"

"Then Mister Crandall, he's from Mister Scott's office in New Orleans, came out of his car. I guess he heard the ruckus, and he come to see what was happening. He tried to pull Rawlings away, but Rawlings pulled a gun. Shot Mister Crandall in the leg. Then he shot Mister Schuster, and all hell broke loose. Men were taking sides, some of them backing Rawlings. They wanted to string us all up. And some of the men got in a big circle around me and Peter and Mister Crandall, who was layin' there bleeding the whole time. And . . ."

"What about Schuster?"

Kinkaid swallowed again, this time harder, and started to blubber a bit. He wiped the shiny ooze creeping down over his upper lip, the track of an invisible snail. "He's dead. . . ."

"And Crandall?"

Kinkaid shrugged. He looked at Shillig. "We don't

know. He was alive when we left, but he was hurt bad, there was a mess of blood and . . .''

"What about Rawlings?" Lex asked. "What did he do then?"

"I don't know. Mister Crandall told us to come get the sheriff. The men were still milling around like scared chickens. I think even the ones that sided with Rawlings were scared then. They knew Mister Schuster was dead, and I guess they was afraid they'd be blamed for it because they sided with the man who done the shooting."

Olson nodded. He tapped his fingertips on his desk top. "I see. Anything else you can think of to tell us?"

Kinkaid shook his head.

"How about you, Mister Shillig. You got anything you want to add?"

"Unh, unh. It's just like he said."

"You said two men had been killed," Lex reminded Kinkaid. "Who was the other one?"

Olson clapped his hand on the desk. "Damn it, Cranshaw, do you mind? This is my office and my job. Why don't you just let me handle it?"

"Rawlings is the reason I'm here, Sheriff. If he's still around, I want him."

"Look, the only sensible thing to do here," Olson said, backing off a little, "is to get a few men together and take a ride out there. I don't rightly expect we'll find Mister Rawlings. Not unless he's a plain fool, but we'll have a looksee. But if he *is* there, then I got dibs on him. If he ain't, then we'll see what's to be done about it. How's that sound?"

Lex took a deep breath. He wasn't going to get

anywhere arguing with Olson, and every minute wasted in pointless dispute was another minute Rawlings had to lengthen his lead. "All right, Sheriff. Let's go."

Olson stood up. "Kinkaid, you and Mister Shillig here'll have to come with us. We'll need somebody out there who knows what happened, and if Crandall didn't make it, somebody'll have to look out for the railroad's business until they can send somebody to take charge."

Kinkaid looked at Shillig, clapped his hands on his knees hard enough to send little mushrooms of dust spurting into the still air, and got to his feet. "All right, Sheriff. Whatever you say."

"Fine. You gents just wait here a couple minutes until I can round up a few fellers to ride with us, and we'll get started. Cranshaw, you want to ask them any more questions, you be my guest. I'll be right back."

When Olson was gone, Lex sat down behind his desk. "Mister Kinkaid, you hear any rumors about Rawlings? Among the men, I mean?"

"No, nothing. He was a bit of a bully. But that's not uncommon. Work crews aren't exactly the cream of the crop, you know. He had a few scrapes, but there wasn't a day we didn't have some sort of trouble, mostly fistfights and such. A couple of times somebody got cut, mostly when there was whiskey around. But Rawlings wasn't no worse than anybody else in that regard."

"He have any friends among the men?"

Kinkaid shrugged. "I suppose so. It's only natural, you're out in the middle of nowhere, you kind of look for somebody to play cards with, somebody to drink with, that sort of thing."

"Anybody close enough to him they might run with him?"

"What do you mean?"

"I mean, if Rawlings took off, was there anybody likely to take off with him? Man's gonna run for his life, he likes to have company. Especially out here. There's all kinds of trouble. Comanche and Kiowa bands out on the plains, bandits. A man'd be smart to bring an extra hand or two along with him, wouldn't you think?"

"I guess. The only way to be sure, though, is to have a roll call. We do that every day anyhow, to make sure our records are accurate. We can do that when we get there, if you want."

"I do. Anything else you can think of? Did Rawlings have any particular reason to dislike Mister Schuster?"

"Management is never popular with working men, Mister Cranshaw. I'm sure you understand that. They always want to work less and get paid more. But Mister Schuster didn't have anything to do with payroll. He was just in charge of the engineering."

Olson barged in before Lex could frame another question. "Let's get to it," he said. "Got half a dozen men to ride with us. I reckon we can handle just about anything we're likely to run into. They probably all sitting around like naughty children right now. That's the way it usually happens. But we'll see."

ON THE ride out to the work camp, Roy Childress attached himself to Lex. Cranshaw looked at the motley assortment of ranch hands and the two railroad men from time to time, wondering how it could end any way but badly. Lute Olson seemed like he was on the way to a picnic, and it occurred to Lex that, other than filling his drunk tank on a payday weekend, the sheriff probably hadn't had much to do in years. If he was as prickly with the work crew as he had been in his office, things were going to get a lot worse before they got better.

And all Lex really wanted was to get his hands on Barton Rawlings and leave Monroe behind as far and as quickly as he could manage it.

"You seem kind of quiet, Lex," Childress said, easing his mount in close to the Ranger. "Somethin' on your mind?"

Lex shook his head. "Just thinking, Roy; is all. Just thinking."

"Ain't much to think about, seems like to me.

Your man is out there, and even if he ain't done what you think he done, we know he killed a man, at least one, this morning. I'd think you'd be kinda glad about that."

"Nothing to be glad about, Roy. Henry Schuster is dead. Maybe Crandall is dead, too. And there was somebody else got shot. Doesn't seem like any reason to throw a party."

"Look at it this way, Lex," Childress said. "Instead of havin' to go in there and clap Rawlings in irons all by your lonesome, you got a lot of help. That'll make it a whole lot easier, I should think. I was you, I'd be smilin' from ear to ear."

"I'll smile when it's over, Roy. And trust me, it's a long, long way from over. More than likely, Rawlings is long gone. And I got to find him. I don't know how long that'll take, but there's no way in hell it's gonna be easier."

"You worry too much, Lex. These boys are good men. I know them a long time. And Sheriff Olson, he's been wearin' a badge a long time. He knows what he's doin'. Between the two of you, I figure you can handle whatever comes along. And if there's gunplay, well, so be it. I'm a pretty fair shot. Won the turkey shoot back home when I was only thirteen. My eyes are still good."

"Men aren't the same as turkeys, Roy. You ever shoot a man?"

"In the war. I done plenty of shootin'. I was at Chancellorsville and Stone Mountain. I don't know how bad it can be, tryin' to tame a pack of gandy dancers, but compared to the war, I'd guess it'd be some better, don't you?"

"Yeah, Roy. It'd be some better." Lex clamped his jaws shut like a bear trap. As often as he'd tried, he knew you couldn't make a man understand that war was different. It was the stuff of cold sweats and urine-soaked pants, for sure, but it was nothing at all like standing ten feet away from a man and looking him in the eye, knowing that in five seconds, or ten, one of you might be dead. And Roy Childress was not going to be the first man to understand that difference.

It was nearly three hours later when the small posse crested a low rise and the thick black smoke of a roaring fire smudged the horizon. "Looks like they set the place ablaze," Olson shouted.

"Hold on, Sheriff," Kinkaid yelled. "That's a work fire. We got to creosote our own ties. They're pushin' the railroad as fast as they can, and the ties come in raw to save time. Nothing to worry about."

"You sure about that, Johnny?"

"Yes, sir, I am."

Olson didn't look convinced, but it had been a long ride and the unforgiving sun was still riding high in the sky. Olson might be fidgety, but he was smart enough to know that the men he was leading were hot and tired. There was no need to push them too hard, not if he wanted to get something out of them when push came to shove.

The men seemed to sense something, and they speeded up, despite Kinkaid's explanation. They were heading for the end-of-track, and they could see puffs of smoke from an engine now, whitish gray in the glaring sunlight. The figures of several men were clustered about a hundred yards ahead of the engine.

They looked like dark gray silhouettes through Lex's squinted eyes.

Kinkaid, feeling more comfortable on familiar turf, moved out ahead of the sheriff, and Shillig, not to be outdone, pushed his own horse behind that of his colleague. Kinkaid dismounted as two men finished pounding a slight mound of dark earth flat with the backs of their shovels.

Olson dismounted and Lex was right behind him. The cowhands, not quite sure what was happening, stayed in their saddles.

"What the hell's goin' on here?" Olson barked.

Lex could see three rectangles of raw earth arranged in a row, two of them already beginning to lighten as the dirt dried under the sun's heat. "Mister Crandall," one of the men with the shovel said, "wanted to be buried under the track."

Kinkaid looked at the sheriff before asking, "Crandall died?"

The man nodded. "About twenty minutes after you left. Said he give his life for this goddamned railroad, he figured he might as well be part of it. We done the same for Mister Schuster and for Alan Keats. Figured we might as well."

"Where's Barton Rawlings?" Lex asked. Olson glared at him, but Lex ignored the sheriff.

"He lit out before Mister Crandall died."

"Which way did he go?"

"Headed west. I reckon he's planning on getting to New Mexico, maybe California."

"Anybody with him?"

The man nodded. "Two fellers. Jim something . . . never did know his name. Everybody just called him Jim or Jimbo. And Bob Meyers. They got a pretty good start, but I reckon we're well rid of 'em anyhow.''

Lex started back to the roan.

"Where you goin', Cranshaw?'' Olson snapped.

"After Rawlings. You can come along if you like.''

"What for? He's long gone. Never find him out there,'' Olson said, waving an arm toward the white sky and bleached-out grass of the plains stretching as far as the eye could see toward the purple smear of the distant Sangre de Cristo Mountains. "Nothing but rattlesnakes and redskins out there. You want him that bad, you be my guest, but I don't reckon I'll be following you. Neither will these fellers.''

"I'll go, Mister Cranshaw,'' Childress offered.

Lex shook his head. "No need, Roy. I don't know how long it'll take.''

"Hell, nothing much to keep me here, Lex. I was pretty well tired of Monroe, anyhow. Might be there's somethin' better waitin' for me.''

"You sure?''

Before he could answer, Olson stepped up to the raw-boned cowhand. "You might want to think it over, Roy. Cranshaw's right. It's his business to run down men like Rawlings. But you don't know a damned thing about it. It's one thing to ride in a posse, but it's a damn sight harder to track a son of a bitch like that across hell. You sure you know what you're doing?''

Childress scratched his cheek, then spat a long amber stream of tobacco juice into the dirt, smeared it to paste with the toe of one boot, then shook his head. "Yeah, I know what I'm doin', Sheriff. Don't worry about it. Just tell Mister Carlisle where I went. Tell him I'll be back in a few days, if he wants to hold my job for me. If not, well, that's okay, too."

"I'll tell him, Roy," Olson said, his voice rich with doubt as to the wisdom of Roy's decision. The sheriff looked at Lex then. "You're gonna go, Cranshaw, you better get a move on. I'll see what these boys can tell me. If you do catch up with him, I expect you'll have to come back this way, and I'd appreciate it if you let me know. Seems only fair that Monroe gets to stake a claim on the bastard."

"I'll be back, Sheriff, one way or the other."

Kinkaid said, "Before you leave, Mister Cranshaw, you'd better let the mess crew fix you some supplies." Lex didn't want to wait, but he knew Kinkaid was right. He hadn't expected to be on the trail again so soon, and there wasn't much in his saddlebags.

"All right, Mister Kinkaid, thank you. Have them pack enough for three men for a few days, would you?"

"Sure thing. Larry, run and tell Cookie to put a pack together. Get a pack horse, too, will you?"

Olson sidled up to Lex. "You sure are goin' to a lot of trouble, Cranshaw. It ain't like you couldn't throw a rock and hit somebody who needs to spend a little time behind bars. What's so important about Rawlings?"

"I told you, Sheriff, he's wanted for murder."

"Yeah, you told me that. But that still don't seem like it's enough for you to go to all this trouble."

"Some things don't bear talking about, Sheriff. This is one of them."

"Whatever you say. But you be careful. And I'll

have the jail cleaned out, just in case you get lucky. We'll have a nice neat little cell waiting for Mister Rawlings. If he makes it back, that is."

"He will. You can bank on it."

"Don't let Roy, here, step on his own feet. He's likely to get hisself killed, he ain't careful."

Lex nodded. He couldn't quite get a fix on Olson. The man seemed anxious to have Rawlings brought back, but not anxious enough to help do it. And right now there was no time to get the sheriff to be more forthcoming.

Kinkaid moved closer, and said, "Better come with me, Mister Cranshaw. You can tell Cookie what you need."

Lex excused himself and followed Kinkaid down past the chuffing engine to the small tent city the work crew called home. He could see several wagons, obviously used to store supplies, arranged in a tight circle beyond the clustered tents.

"Looks more like a military camp than a work camp, Mister Kinkaid," Lex observed.

The railroad man nodded. "Never know what you're likely to run into out here. We had more than our share of Indian troubles in the past, and it pays to be careful. Nothing major, you understand, but there are more than a few Comanche bands still out there."

Kinkaid waved a hand to encompass a broad circle. Instinctively, Lex followed the gesture. The world seemed an empty wasteland with the small camp at its heart. As far as he could see in any direction, there was nothing but the rolling hills and the sun-blanched grass, most of it too brittle even to rustle in the dry, hot wind.

"Kiowas, too," Kinkaid added. "Supposed to be on reservations, all of 'em, but some of 'em haven't heard, and some of those who have don't give a good god damn. And there's more than a few redskins use the reservation as a base camp. Slip away when they feel like, raise some havoc, and tuck their tails between their legs and run for home when the heat gets too much for 'em. I was you, Mister Cranshaw, I'd be real careful out there. More than likely, if you find Rawlings, he might not have his hair."

"I can't afford to worry about that, Mister Kinkaid. I have a job to do. If that means taking a chance, then I'll just have to take it."

"I don't know whether to admire you or pity you, Mister Cranshaw."

Lex grinned. "Hardly matters which, if you're right, Mister Kinkaid. And if you're wrong, then I reckon either one would be wasted."

"For your sake, I hope I'm wrong."

"So do I, Mister Kinkaid. So do I. But I have to tell you, I've seen more than my share of ugliness in the last fifteen years. And the worst I've seen had nothing to do with Indians. In my experience, there's nothing uglier than the things some white men are prepared to do to each other. Most of it for pure meanness."

I T HAD been a long ride. Lex Cranshaw was bone tired, sunbaked and dry as a pitcher full of sand. He looked up at the sky, where the sun stared back at him, its gaze blank, bleak as the endless prairie that stretched out ahead of him, bleaching the brittle grass until it looked like straw. Far ahead, three small specks bobbed near the horizon, drawing him on the way one magnet drew another.

Reaching for his canteen, he unscrewed the cap, raised its metal mouth to his lips and felt the grit of salts accumulated in the threaded spout as he tipped it back enough to fill his mouth with tepid water. For a moment, he thought he had filled his mouth with dust. He felt the water making a thick paste of the trail dust, spat the glutinous mess into the grass and took another mouthful of water.

This time, he rinsed the sandy grit, spat a thin stream off to the side, then took one final mouthful, swallowed it, and screwed the lid back on. Looping the canteen over his saddle horn by its leather strap, Lex looked at the sun once more. He would have given a month's pay for a single cloud, a year's pay for a cloudburst.

The big roan stallion beneath him plodded on as if it were impervious to the blazing sun. And far ahead, the black specks, the only reason he was out there in the middle of nowhere, continued to dance in the brilliant glare. His quarry, and the black specks were nothing more or less than that, seemed oblivious of their pursuers.

Lex stabbed a finger, and Roy Childress squinted in the glare. "See them, Roy?"

Childress shook his head. "Sort of. I guess. I swear, Mister Cranshaw, if I'd a known how you earned your pay, I think I'd have been a little more respectful."

"It's not all like this, Roy."

"Maybe not, but a little of this goes a long way. You figure we're gonna catch up to them soon?"

"By nightfall, I hope. As long as they don't know we're here, we should be able to close the gap. After dark, if we're lucky, we might be able to get close enough to move in on them."

"I sure as hell hope so."

Lex realized he just might be counting unhatched chickens. But when he glanced once more at the baleful, unblinking eye of the sun overhead, he knew that he didn't have much choice. If he didn't make a move soon, Rawlings and company would be over the line and gone.

And there was no way on God's green earth that he was going to come this far, under these conditions, and ride back to Monroe empty-handed. Rawlings was giving him a good run, but in the end, it was going to come up short.

"Bank on it, Mister Rawlings," Lex whispered.

He looked over his shoulder, as if to tally the miles he'd ridden in the last few days, and nodded, almost as if he thought that Major Earl Podell was watching him. The Texas Rangers were like that, tied together, tied to their commanding officers, tied to the notion of law enforcement that men like Lee Hall and Jack Hays had refined with such precision that it resembled a religion more nearly than it resembled anything else.

And Lex Cranshaw was a true believer. A country as big and as empty as Texas had room enough for any man bold enough, or damn fool enough, to want to stake a claim to her. And that limitless expanse was all the more reason why one man ought to respect another, let him live his life without interference. Texas was a place where you could come after you'd run out of options everyplace else. You could burn down your house, shoot the dog, saddle up and ride south. There wouldn't be a band to welcome you at the state line, but there sure as hell would be plenty of room for you to bury your past and start fresh.

But with all that room, there still seemed not to be enough for some men—men like Barton Rawlings. Rawlings had ridden into the jerkwater town of McComas, gone to the bank, and made a withdrawal of eight hundred dollars, despite the fact that he had no account, and that had been only the beginning. And now, two years, nine banks, five thousand eight hundred and seventy-three dollars, and three dead bankers later, Rawlings was headed for New Mexico. After a stop along the way that resulted in three more dead men. And that was history no one could bury

deep enough—not as long as there were men like
Lex Cranshaw to see to it.

Lex and Childress had been following as close as
they dared for a day and a half, but Rawlings was
smart, and he was desperate. Reluctant to move in
on him at night, for fear he might lose him altogether, Lex had been content to tag along, hoping
for Rawlings to make a mistake. But so far, Rawlings
had been perfect.

Pushing the big roan to its limits, Lex drove on,
watching the flyspecks of Barton Rawlings and his
cronies fade in and out of sight as they moved
through the gently rolling hills. But soon, too soon for
Lex's liking, Rawlings would reach the edge of the
Sangre de Cristo Mountains. Once he made it into
that bewildering maze of canyons and gullies, dry
washes and rocky draws, he would be as good as
gone.

It was nearly six in the afternoon when Lex reined
in and reached for his field glasses. He wanted to get
a better look at Rawlings before sundown. Two miles
wasn't much in open country, but that would change
the following day, and if Lex was going to move in,
and if he expected to run him down, this would have
to be the night. He had no choice.

Even through the glasses, the watery shimmer of
the late afternoon sun made it hard to pick out the
big man. If it were not for Rawlings's penchant for
bright red shirts, which he had worn in all of the bank
robberies, and ever since Lex had gotten onto his tail,
Rawlings would have blended in with the terrain. The
mix of earth tones—browns from beige to umber—
and some greens sun-faded and running to gray,

made it easy for a man to hide himself if that's what he wanted to do.

But Rawlings didn't seem to give a damn. The whole time Lex had been on his trail, he had not made one attempt to throw off pursuit. He had broken out of the railroad work camp at a dead gallop, and headed straight as an arrow ever since. Whether he was daring Lex to close on him, or totally oblivious to the possibility that someone might be on his trail, Lex couldn't decide.

It was nearly eight o'clock when Rawlings finally reached the first rocky draws of the Sangre de Cristo foothills. And almost nine before Lex had felt comfortable with the idea of getting in close.

Just as the sun had gone down, smearing the sky with blotches of purple and slicing them in two with blades of orange, Rawlings had headed into the mouth of a canyon. Common sense told Lex that his quarry had gone to ground for the night. And that same common sense told him that Rawlings would open his bedroll next in the Territory of New Mexico.

Heading into the canyon with Roy Childress by his side was only slightly less risky than heading in alone, and since there was little to choose, he had told Childress to stay close and keep quiet.

Lex crept through the narrow canyon. A couple of hundred yards ahead, he could see the faint wash of orange light where the glow from Rawlings's campfire spilled around one last turn before surrendering to the maze.

The Ranger was beginning to wonder whether Rawlings had met someone, or simply felt that he was safe enough to risk the comfort of a hot meal and a cup of coffee. It was the first time in three days Rawlings had built a fire. Pressing flat against the towering rock wall to his right, Lex inched forward, careful to place each boot securely before moving the next. One misstep could alert his quarry and cost him his last opportunity to make the capture.

Straining his ears, Lex could hear nothing. He kept watching the smeared light on the towering cliff across the way. If Rawlings were to hear something and come looking, Lex's only warning might be a shadow on the opposite wall. So far, so good. A small brook trickled through the sandy bottom, an occasional rock making it mutter, but that had been the only sound.

After twenty yards, the orange light was much brighter. Lex was following the twisting wall, staying as flat against it as he could, his Winchester beginning to feel slippery in his left hand. Taking a deep breath, he ducked under the scrawny trunk of a scrub oak clinging precariously to the stony face of the canyon not more than five feet off the ground.

When he straightened, he heard the sharp crack of stone on stone and froze. The sound had come from somewhere ahead, just around the bend. He listened intently, thinking perhaps Rawlings had heard him and was heading his way. Dropping to one knee, he thumbed back the hammer on the Winchester, just in case.

Turning to look over his shoulder, he could just make out the angular shape of Roy Childress, awkward as a crippled stork, groping along the wall fifteen yards behind. So far the cowboy hadn't made a sound. If only that luck would hold, Lex just might pull it off.

There was no further sound for several seconds. Then Lex heard the nicker of a horse and the muffled thud of hooves on sand. "Shut up, Rascal," someone said.

It dawned on Lex that he had no idea what Barton Rawlings sounded like, and that there was no way for him to know whether it was Rawlings who had spoken or someone else. The only thing he could do was assume that Rawlings and his two followers were not alone. And that changed everything, especially the odds.

Dropping to the ground, Lex wormed ahead, staying as close to the base of the wall as he could. Clumps of weeds sprouted among the broken rock, but there was no brush and no cover worth a damn, except for the wall itself.

The horse nickered again, but this time no one said anything. After crawling about fifty feet, Lex stopped once more to listen. He could hear the rattle of metal on metal, probably the scrape of a fork on a tin plate. He heard the crackle of exploding sap, and saw the rush of light as the flames climbed a little higher for a few moments.

Rawlings and his men apparently had nothing to say to each other. Lex rolled to his left once, then over again, trying to get far enough away from the base of the wall to see past the outcrop of red rock a few yards ahead. Once more, he heard the thud of hooves on the sandy bottom.

Starting ahead again, he heard the sharp crack of one stone on another, then the clatter as it rolled away. For a long moment, he held his breath, wondering whether the rock had been kicked by someone or simply fallen from the canyon wall. Once more, one of the mounts nickered. The horse was nervous about something, and it didn't take much for it to prick up its ears.

Letting his breath out in a slow stream between pursed lips, Lex fingered the Winchester anxiously. He signaled to Childress to come ahead and was about to get to his feet and charge into the open when he heard the clatter of tin once more. Then footsteps. Someone was on the move, but Lex couldn't be certain in what direction.

Getting to his feet cautiously, he brought the Winchester around, bracing it against his hip. The thump of the feet was receding now, as if the man were walking farther into the canyon. Lex took a few steps forward, then moved to the right and pressed himself up against the sharp-edged outcrop of brittle rock.

Waving Childress on, he waited until the cowhand joined him, and leaned close to whisper in his ear, "Somebody's moving around. I'm going to try to get a look."

Childress nodded that he understood. Leaning to the left, Lex peered around the corner. He could see the fire now and beyond it Rawlings's black, unsaddled and tethered near the edge of the brook, where the animal could graze on the tufts of lush grass and drink all it wanted. Two more horses bobbed their heads a few yards away.

Lex saw Rawlings kneel at the water's edge, then lean forward to rinse his plate in the sluggish water. Someone called to him, and the big man turned around, straightening but staying on his knees. Lex hesitated in the limbo of indecision, uncertain whether to plunge ahead or wait to see what happened. As long as the campfire continued to burn, there would be light enough, even in the bowels of the canyon. And if he held his water just a bit, maybe an hour, maybe a little more, he could cut down on the risk of a gunfight.

With Childress along, the odds weren't impossible, but if he could get close while the men were sleeping, he could thumb back the hammer and stick a gun in Rawlings's ear before the man knew what was happening.

And they had to be exhausted. Two days of running flat out would drain the sap out of any man. Lex was already dragging, and he was probably a lot more used to the rigors of the trail than Rawlings, and certainly than Roy Childress.

He sucked in a breath and held it, watching Rawlings get to his feet and walk back toward the fire, a long shadow spilling on the ground behind him. He'd found his man. There was no point in throwing away the one last chance he might have.

"Patience," he whispered, "just a little patience."

THE WAIT was killing him, but Lex bided his time. Childress seemed just as happy to sit on his hands, as if he were having second thoughts about having volunteered. The cowhand's face was drawn, and there was a knot of muscle bunched in the corner of his jaw.

The fire died slowly. Gradually, the orange light on the canyon walls began to weaken, and the shadows in the crevices seemed to be oozing out like some dark fluid, threatening to swallow everything. Overhead, the stars were clearly visible, and Lex kept watching them, waiting for the right time, as if he expected to read some signal there. Once, a meteor speared across the darkness, leaving a lingering trace of its passage as if it had rent the sky like a dark cloth and allowed white light to seep through from the other side. But soon that light, too, faded away.

Every time there was a sound, Childress jumped. Twice, Lex had to grab him and clamp a hand over his mouth to keep him from crying out. Each time,

Childress looked embarrassed, shaking his head and shaping apologetic words on his trembling lips.

Then, finally, it was time. There was nothing to be gained by delaying any longer. If Rawlings wasn't asleep yet, he would never be. Telling Childress to stay put, he got to his feet, worked a shell into the Winchester's chamber and started around the bend.

Childress took a couple of tentative steps after him, as if he didn't want to be left alone, but Lex waved him back. They had already decided how to play it. Lex wanted to take the initiative, leaving Childress as a hole card of uncertain value.

Once he turned the corner, he could see three shapes arranged in a row a few feet from the fire that had diminished to a few flickering tongues and a shaky plume of gray smoke. The horses had settled down, and Lex moved forward in a crouch. It was tempting to open fire and fill the three men with lead. There were some Rangers, he knew, who would have played it that way. And there were times when he wished he could be one of them. But he wasn't made that way. Fair play still meant something to him, even though it seemed increasingly scarce a commodity.

He wasn't sure which of the three sleeping men was Rawlings, but he knew the big man was the key. More than likely, the two others were nothing more than hangers-on. They would take their cue from Rawlings and if Lex took him out of action, the others would fold easily. Or so Lex hoped.

Thumbing back the Winchester's hammer, he tiptoed closer, forcing his eyes to stay wide open, trying to freeze the sleeping men in place until he was close enough to stick the muzzle of the Winchester in the nearest ear.

At twenty-five feet, one of the men moaned and rolled over. For a moment, Lex froze. He thought he'd seen the white of an eye, but the man gave a loud, shuddering snore, and settled back down. It wasn't Rawlings, which meant his quarry was either the man in the middle or the one at the far end of the short line.

Circling around the fire, he inched closer and closer, holding his breath now. Leaning forward, he reached out with the Winchester, poked the shoulder of the sleeping middle man, then backed away as the man grunted, brushed at the shoulder then sat up abruptly.

"Just take it nice and easy," Lex whispered.

But the man didn't listen. He shouted something that came so suddenly and echoed so immediately that its meaning was lost. But the sleepers on either side of him bolted up.

Lex fired once, aiming high, hoping the sudden thunder of the rifle shot would stun them for a moment into motionlessness. It didn't work.

The man on the right grabbed for something and Lex fired again even before he knew what it was. Once more, he tried not to hit the men, and his bullet slammed into the campfire, shattering the last substantial log and sending a fan of sparks in every direction. Tiny embers drifted up and winked like fireflies before going out. Whatever the man had been reaching for no longer seemed like a good idea and he raised his hands over his head and turned toward Lex, his eyes trying to blink away the sleep that bound them as surely as if they had been coated with mucilage.

Lex heard footsteps from behind him and knew that Childress was coming. He only hoped the cowboy didn't do something stupid.

"Stand easy," Lex said, this time barking the words so sharply they echoed off the canyon walls. "You're under arrest."

Rawlings shook his head, as if he couldn't believe he'd been taken so easily. "Who the hell are you, cowboy?" he asked.

"Name's Cranshaw," Childress said, his confidence resurgent. "He's a Texas Ranger. Tracked you all the way from Monroe."

Rawlings spat. "Go to hell! No way I'm going back. You might as well shoot me now, because there's no way in hell I'm going back."

"You're going back, all right, Rawlings. You can take that to the bank. And for a change, you can make a deposit, instead of a withdrawal."

"We'll see about that." Rawlings smiled.

"Roy," Lex snapped, "pat him down. But be careful." Lex stepped between Rawlings and his two companions, neither of whom had said a word.

"Yes, sir, Mister Cranshaw. It'll be a natural pleasure." Childress set his rifle down carefully, then walked toward Rawlings and stepped around behind him. He gave him a cursory frisk, patting Rawlings's pockets. Then, backing away, he said, "He's not carryin' nothing."

Lex looked at the two other captives. "What are your names?" he asked.

One of them bore a striking resemblance to Barton Rawlings, although he was three or four inches shorter and thirty pounds lighter than Rawlings's six one and two hundred. The Rawlings look-alike shook his head. "Go to hell." He was a sound-alike, as well.

"Have it your way, gents. But I have to tell you that since Henry Schuster, Thomas Crandall, and Alan Keats were murdered yesterday morning by Mister Rawlings, here, and since you appear to be accomplices in those murders, I have no choice but to charge you with those crimes. You can either talk to me or you can talk to the judge."

The other man, rail thin and unnaturally pale under a recent sunburn, narrowed his black eyes to slits. "You can't charge me with nothing. I ain't done nothing and you can't prove otherwise."

"You can hope so, mister," Lex said. "But there were plenty of witnesses. I don't imagine it'll take much to round a few of them up. Once they start talking, I figure the judge won't be too sympathetic. You got anything to say, you better say it now."

The thin man shook his head. "Ain't saying nothing. Nothing at all."

"Have it your way, then." Turning to Childress, Lex said, "Roy, check their tack. There must be some rope we can use to tie them up. No sense moving out before morning."

Childress bobbed his head, eager as a schoolboy, and spun in a circle, looking for the saddles. Spotting one at the head of one of the bedrolls, he sprinted toward it, squatted to loosen a coiled lariat, and dashed back to his position behind Rawlings.

"Tie his hands behind his back, Roy. Make sure it's tight."

Childress jerked a knife from its sheath on his hip, measured a pair of six-foot lengths of rope and sawed them off. Dropping the coils, he grabbed Rawlings by the arm, pulled it backward, and Rawlings jerked it back the other way, pulling Childress off balance. Before Lex could stop him, Rawlings snaked an arm around the cowboy's neck, squeezing the windpipe with a thick forearm. At the same time, he twisted Childress's wrist, forcing him to drop the knife.

The thin man dove for his gear, and Lex swung the Winchester around, trying to get a bead on him. Rawlings retrieved the knife and had the blade at Roy's throat.

Lex fired, and the thin man bucked, his body bowing as if he'd been kicked in the stomach.

The small Rawlings look-alike had started for his own gun, but stopped, bent at the waist and nearly falling over as he tried to regain his balance, his hands slowly rising above his head.

"You want me to slit him from ear to ear, you just hang on to that rifle," Rawlings said. "Otherwise, you'd best put it down."

"How far do you think you'll get, Rawlings?" Lex asked. He eased a little closer to the smaller man, disguising it as an attempt to relax the tension. Leaning on the Winchester, its butt on the ground, he curled his fingers around the barrel.

"Far as I want to," Rawlings sneered. "Course, you fellas won't be in no shape to follow me, and I

don't guess anybody else will know or care. So . . .''
He shrugged.

Lex eased a little closer to the small man. "What
you're saying is, I give up the gun, you kill us both. I
don't give it up, you just kill Roy, there, that right?''

Rawlings bobbed his head, but didn't answer. Lex
eased another half step closer. "Of course, you kill
him, then I kill you. Seems like a Mexican standoff, at
best. But then I'm still breathing and you aren't.
Sounds like a bad gamble to me. I don't like the odds
your way.''

"Drop the damn rifle. Do it now!'' Rawlings's
voice was tight. Lex could see the white knuckles
curled around the handle of Roy's knife.

"Maybe you better do like he says, Mister Cranshaw. He won't hurt us none. Just tie us up and leave
us, ain't that right?'' Roy's voice was quavering, and
he turned his head a bit to try to look Rawlings in the
eye, but the edge of the blade knicked him, and he
winced. Rawlings shifted his weight and Lex took the
one chance he might have.

Swinging the Winchester like a club, he smashed
the butt across the small man's face, catching him on
the bridge of the nose. He heard the sharp crack of
bone, and whirled as the small man went down. Roy,
the strength of desperation suddenly infusing his
gangly frame, drove an elbow into Rawlings's gut and
twisted sideways.

As the air went out of him, Rawlings tried to
double over. The knife sliced into Roy's shoulder, but
he managed to twist free, and Lex sprang toward the
doubled-over Rawlings and brought his boot up in a

sharp arc. The boot caught Rawlings under the chin, its point driving into the killer's throat, and he gagged, then fell to his knees. The knife slipped from his grasp as he brought his hands up to cover his face.

Lex swung the Winchester overhead and slammed the butt down on the back of Rawlings's head. The crash of wood on bone made a hollow thud, like a watermelon being thumped with a knuckle, and Rawlings collapsed.

Lex took a deep breath. "You all right, Childress?" he asked.

Roy, one hand clamped over the bloody gash in his shirt, shook his head. "I don't know. It hurts like a son of a bitch."

"Let me take a look."

Lex had to pry the clamped hand away from the wound. Pulling the bloody edges of the shirt away, he leaned close. "It's clean. Didn't hit the bone. You'll be okay, but we have to get that tended to."

"Ain't no place but Monroe with a doc," Childress moaned. He straightened up and his eyes glazed over as he started to totter. A split second later, he folded like a jackknife and fell to the ground.

Shaking his head, Lex muttered, "Just what I need."

There was some first-aid gear in the pack, but he couldn't leave to get it until he had Rawlings and friends secured. It was looking like a long night as he snatched the pieces of rope Childress had cut and tied Rawlings hand and foot. Cutting two more pieces of rope, he tied the small man, whose face was a bloody mess and who almost certainly had a broken nose.

Moving to the third, he set the rope down, the knife beside it, then knelt to feel for a pulse.

There was none.

THEY HAD buried the dead man without knowing his name because Barton Rawlings refused to identify him. After piling the last stone in place on the makeshift cairn, Roy Childress had wanted to say a little prayer, but when he asked Rawlings for the man's name, all he'd say was "He's dead. What difference does it make? Let him rot."

The smaller version, whom Lex was convinced must be Rawlings's brother, had seemed on the verge of answering the question, but a glare from the big man had snapped his jaw shut with the finality of a bear trap.

So Roy said his prayer without mentioning any names. "You know who he is, Lord, and we ask that you forgive him," Childress had said. Rawlings had stood by chuckling, his hands tied behind his back.

Lex had scowled at him, but Rawlings had just smiled. "Tell you what," he said, "when I come back this way, I'll put a little sign over his bones, if it'll make you feel better. I know it ain't gonna help him none."

The ride back took three days. Lex had kept thinking about it the whole way back to Monroe, but all it did was make him mad, and he kept trying to push the thought out of his mind. And every time he did, he could hear that nasty chuckle of Barton Rawlings, "He's dead. Let him rot."

More than once, it crossed his mind that the best thing might just be to put a bullet in Rawlings's head and let *him* rot. It would save the State of Texas the cost of a trial, and there wasn't much chance that anyone would ever know or care. But Lex wasn't made that way. There was the Texas way, and there was the right way. Maybe it was his Kentucky roots, with the slight veneer of gentility, maybe it was some innate decency that wouldn't let him descend to the level of the men he spent his life chasing, and maybe it was the possibility of standing there in the crowd to watch Rawlings stretch a rope, his feet dangling as he spun a few feet off the ground, urine staining his pants and dripping from the downturned toes of his boots. But whatever it was, Barton Rawlings was still alive when Monroe came into view once more.

Somebody must have spotted the small party and guessed who it was because by the time they reached the edge of town there was a small crowd gathered in front of the sheriff's office. Lute Olson was standing in the doorway, his feet spread wide, his wiry arms folded across his chest.

He nodded, a slight smile twisting his salt-and-pepper mustache into a shallow U shape. "Brung him in, did you, Cranshaw?" he asked.

Lex slid from the saddle and tied up before answering. When he did, it was only to ignore the question. "Roy needs a doctor to look at his shoulder. Somebody run and get him, would you?"

The cowhands looked at Childress, then gathered around his horse. "What happened, Roy, you fall down?" one asked.

Another shook his head and clapped Childress on the thigh. "Naw, Roy prob'ly shot hisself, ain't that right, Roy?"

Childress grinned good-naturedly and swung one long leg up over his saddle horn. "Get out of the way, Schuyler; Jesus, let a man git down from his horse, would ya?"

He dropped to the ground, grinning from ear to ear. "You boys thought I was crazy, didn't you? Thought there was no way in hell we'd ever find this sumbitch, didn't you? But we found him, and we brung him back, where he can stretch a rope nice and proper like."

" 'Fraid not, Roy," Lex said. "You can have the little one, whoever the hell he is, but Rawlings is my prisoner, and we'll be moving on tomorrow." Turning to Olson, he said, "Sheriff, I'd appreciate the loan of a cell for the night, if you don't mind."

Olson tilted his head back a little and rocked on his heels. "Seems to me like we got a claim on this here feller our ownselves, Mister Cranshaw. You want him, you'd best think about finding someplace else to put him."

"You know you're obligated to cooperate, don't you, Sheriff?" Lex asked.

"Hell, I'll cooperate. I'll even introduce you to Matt

Harbaugh, runs the hotel. Maybe he'll even give you a break on the rate.''

Lex shook his head. "I don't think that'll be good enough, Sheriff.''

Olson swaggered a bit, then took a step forward and dropped off the boardwalk, landing on his heels. "Hells bells, Cranshaw. Relax, why don't you. I was just havin' some fun at your expense. Course you can have a cell. You can have two, if you want to keep these boys separate. Who's the other one, by the way?''

"I don't know. He won't say, and neither will Rawlings.''

"He kinda favors Rawlings a bit, don't he? Could be a kid brother or something. Course, with his nose all mashed up like it is, I ain't sure even his mother would know him.''

"Your guess is as good as mine, Sheriff.''

"Well, let's haul their asses inside and introduce 'em to Monroe hospitality. A couple years down the road, after that railroad goes through, we'll probably have more comfortable surroundings for 'em. But I don't think it'll make much difference. Mister Rawlings don't seem like the type to care much for civilized accommodations.''

Lex reached up to help the smaller man from the saddle. The prisoner's face was still badly swollen, and both eyes were blackened. The cheeks beneath them were a jaundiced yellow blending into purple and dark blue.

Olson noticed the bruises and looked at them with something akin to admiration. "Looks like he ran into a wall," he said. "Had some help from you on that, I reckon." He laughed, and the cowboys gathered around chuckled with him.

Rawlings was hustled off his horse by several pairs of hands, and the cowboys were none too gentle in getting him down. One gave him a shove, and Rawlings stumbled as he tried to negotiate the step up onto the boardwalk, missed, and barked his shins on the rough timbers as he went down.

With a snarl, he turned on his back and lashed out with a boot, catching the nearest cowhand in the knee. The crack of heel on bone brought a groan from the surprised hand, and his leg went out from under him. He landed knee first on Rawlings's midsection, then swung one bony fist, but Lex got there in time to intercept the punch before it landed.

"That's enough," Lex snapped. "You just get the hell away from him. This isn't a circus."

"Sumbitch don't deserve no more'n a rope," the cowboy muttered. "What're you takin' his side for?"

"He's my prisoner," Lex said. "And nobody mistreats a man in my custody. You understand that?"

The man mumbled something Lex didn't catch. The Ranger stepped toward him, grabbed him by the shirt and jerked him forward, despite the fact that the cowboy was two or three inches taller and outweighed Lex by twenty pounds. "What did you say?" Lex barked.

"Nothin'," the man said, squirming in Lex's grasp. "I didn't say nothing. Leggo of my shirt."

Lex gave him a shove, and he stumbled backward a step or two before another cowboy grabbed his arm until he could regain his balance. Turning to the sheriff, Lex said, "I think maybe we should get these men inside before things get out of control."

Olson grinned. "I was kind of lookin' forward to some excitement, Cranshaw. Monroe can get pretty boring these long, hot summers." He saw that Lex was not amused and raised a placatory hand. "Just jokin', " he said. "Don't get all in a lather, now."

Lex hauled Rawlings to his feet, and the big man hissed, "Don't think that cuts any ice with me, Cranshaw. I get a chance, I'm still gonna cut me a piece of your gizzard. Might even toast it with onions."

"You won't get a chance, Rawlings. First thing in the morning, you and I are going to head for Austin. What happens then, I don't give a damn, but I can tell you one thing, if they don't hang you, and I ever run into you again, I'll kill you. Understand?"

Rawlings laughed as Olson prodded him in the gut and he backed up carefully, turned and stepped onto the boardwalk. The little man was already standing by the door, Roy Childress beside him with one hand hooked through his tied arms.

Olson led the way into his office, then slipped back to the doorway after Lex and Rawlings followed him in. "Mister Cranshaw is startin' to get a bad opinion of you boys. Why don't you just run along. Everything's under control here."

There were some shouts of derision, but Olson didn't stay to argue. He backed into the office and closed the door. Hooking a large key ring from a hat rack on the wall, he led the way into the cell block to the right of his desk. The keys jangled almost musically, then clattered against a lock as Lex stepped through the doorway into the block.

Six cells, either a relic of a former prosperity or a wasted symbol of hope for a prosperous future, were arranged in sets of three on either side of the wide corridor. The place smelled dry and musty, as if it had been closed up for years. None of the cells was occupied, and the floor was dusty enough to show smudges where boots had scraped over it since the last time it had been swept out.

Olson, as if he sensed what was on Lex's mind, said, "Place doesn't get much use these days. Worst we get is an occasional drunk, and most times I can just let him sleep it off upstairs over the saloon. It's almost an honor to have a prisoner or two for a change, real prisoners, that is."

Childress escorted the smaller of the two captives into the first open cell, backed out, and Olson ground the key in the lock. "Don't you go nowhere, now," Childress said, laughing. The prisoner glared at him, his face raccoonlike and comical with the mask of blackened eyes and bulging cheeks.

Rawlings lashed out again with a foot and caught Childress in the back of the knee, collapsing the leg and sending the cowboy to the floor.

Childress came up cursing, but Olson beat him to it, cracking his pistol against the side of Rawlings's head and knocking him to his knees. "No call to be uncivilized," he said.

Rawlings was stunned, but not out, and he glared at Olson, tried to get to his feet and when the sheriff raised the pistol overhead, threatening to hit him again, the big man spat. But Olson kept his composure, dodged the gob and brushed on by to open the cell catty-corner to that holding the smaller man.

"Might as well keep these boys separated as much as we can," he said. "Who knows what mischief they might cook up."

"You got anybody to watch them? There a night man, Sheriff?"

"No. No money for that. But these cells are about as secure as you could want. And that there door to the office would hold a mad bear with no trouble. I don't think you have to worry. I'll get a couple of the boys to stay out front if you want."

"I think that would be a good idea," Lex answered.

Childress and the Ranger dragged Rawlings, still on his knees, to the open cell, hauled him inside, and turned him loose. When they left the cell, Olson locked it. "You boys want your hands free, you can stick 'em through the bars and I'll cut them ropes. Otherwise, you can sleep as is. It's all the same to me."

Turning to Lex, he said, "I know you're takin' Rawlings with you, but what about the other one?"

Lex shrugged. "Can't say. I don't know who he is, and I got no reason to hold him. As far as I know, the only crime he's connected with is the shootings at the T and W work camp. That's your jurisdiction, and if you want him, you can have him."

Olson shook his head. "It's all the same to me, Cranshaw. I can send somebody to the county seat and make arrangements for the circuit judge to pay us a visit. Used to come pretty regular, but since Monroe's so tame these days, he waits to hear from us, now."

"We can talk about it in the morning, if you want to sleep on it."

"I'll do that." He led them out of the cell block, locked the heavy door, and returned the key ring to the hat rack.

"What about those cowboys, Sheriff?" Lex asked.

"What about them?"

"They going to make trouble?"

Olson shook his head. "Not really. They're a little bored, is all. But it ain't like they had any connection with the men who got killed. No reason for them to make trouble."

"Can you recommend a place to stay?"

"Sure. See Marty Paich at The Wet Whistle. He's got rooms to let upstairs, and he ain't exactly doing a land-office business, if you know what I mean."

Lex thanked him and walked outside, Childress right behind him, like a cocker spaniel puppy. "See you in the morning before you go, Mister Cranshaw?"

"Sure thing, Roy. And thanks for your help."

"It wasn't nothing."

"You better have the doctor look at that shoulder. You don't want to get infected."

"I will. Maybe I'll see you at dinner later?"

"Maybe."

LEX CLOSED the door to his room, removed his gun belt and coiled it, then set it on the floor right beside the bed. Without bothering to take off his boots, he lay down and took a deep breath. He remembered being this tired only once before in his life. Closing his eyes, he found himself drifting, almost as if he had fallen into some swift current, and whatever lined either bank was little more than a blur as he tumbled over and over and over. And he knew where he was going.

Shiloh.

Slowly shapes began to materialize again, as if a thick fog were slowly burning off under the heat of some so far invisible but unrelenting sun. He could feel the clamminess on his skin, smell the sour mud that coated his arms. The rain hissed as it swirled around him. He tried to roll over onto his back, but could only manage to get on his side. The trees, not yet fully leaved so early in the season, were like pencil sketches against the pale gray sky.

Off in the distance, he could hear the crackle of

gunfire. An occasional rebel yell would slice through the unremitting rain like a white hot knife, then it would die away, there would be more gunfire, and then only the hiss of rain again.

His shoulder throbbed, and he could feel the swelling, feel the ooze of blood under his muddy shirt, feel the wound as surely as if someone were poking him with a sharp stick. He groaned and opened his eyes for a moment, half expecting to see those same trees, but the room was dark. He didn't know how long he'd been sleeping, but he knew that he could sleep forever and still not stop dreaming about the agony of those three days.

Even now, floating in the no-man's-land between sleeping and waking, it was all clear. Individual images came back to him, sharply focused, almost framed like some Brady photographs he had seen once in St. Louis, fragments of time frozen forever, all movement arrested so that the scream of horror still vibrated in the larynx of a man who'd lost a leg to a Yankee cannonball. A man with a sword held high overhead, tumbling backward off his horse, the silver mane crisply waving like a flag as one fist curled into it, bunching the stiff hairs in one last grasp at life, hung suspended forever falling and never touching down. A young boy, a Yankee whose name he would never know, was reaching for his right eyeball as it tumbled down his cheek, blown out by a minié ball, the impact captured a split second later, so that a halo of blood splattering away from the ugly black hole in his temple was motionless in space. But unlike the Brady photographs, these frozen moments were not black and white, they were painted with the full palette of gore.

Lex sat up, knowing that the dreams would come if he were to close his eyes, and knowing that he could not hold sleep off much longer. Maybe, he thought, it would be better to surrender, let the dreams wash over him. Maybe this time he would dream them away and know when he awoke that they would never come back again to haunt him. But he shook his head. He had tried that before a dozen times, a hundred times. But always they came back. They were a part of him now, a part of his life, a life that would have been snuffed out a long time ago, there in a muddy ditch by the side of the road.

But someone he never got to thank had changed all that. She had no reason to care whether he lived or died. In fact, it was a wonder that she didn't kill him herself. He was, after all, fighting on the wrong side as far as she was concerned, on the side that had made her a slave and, if given its chance, would keep her a slave, and her children and theirs as well. But she had not seen the color of his uniform, or the color of his skin, only the color of his blood.

And she had saved him. It had changed him forever, although he had not known it then. And even now, he knew, he did not know the full extent of that change. He knew only that she had given him back something that had not been his to begin with. She had dug in her heels and hauled him back from the brink of death, a precipice over which he had begun to slide into a yawning black emptiness that seemed so seductive and promised such immediate and permanent peace. At first, he had not wanted to come back, and kicked and scratched, trying to force her to let him go.

But she had been a determined woman, and she had prevailed. And one day she had gone out and not come back. He never saw her again, and learned only that she had been struck by a minié ball. Her grandson, who gave him the news, did not even know which side had fired the fatal shot, and professed that it made no difference. She was gone, and that was the one indisputable and only pertinent fact. "Miss Ellie," he whispered. "Miss Ellie."

And her name on his weary lips seemed to soothe him. He lay back again, staring at the pale gray block of light that was the window. It was almost dark now, and a deep shadow seemed to be filling the room, as if it were slowly welling up through cracks in the floorboards, threatening to swallow him as certainly as any flood.

But he no longer cared. He was tired, he wanted to sleep, and he was willing to face those demons if that's what it would take. He closed his eyes, listening to the faint sounds of laughter far down the street, the tinkle of a piano somewhere below him, and, far louder and far closer, the beating of his own heart, pounding against his ribs like a wild beast that had to be free or die.

He took a deep breath.

And slept.

He woke twice during the night, and the darkness soothed him. The second time, he walked to the window and pulled the curtain aside. The street below was empty of everything but moonlight, which turned the dirt to silver. Rolling a cigarette, he sat on the windowsill and struck a match, sucked the smoke eagerly into his lungs, and let it out in a long, thin feather that changed from gray to white as it drifted out into the night.

He wondered about Barton Rawlings, what made a man so indifferent to human life, so callous that he could stand by impassively when a man who had helped him was slowly covered by rocks and sent off into his final rest without even a mention of his name.

There were so many things that Lex didn't understand, not just about the violent world in which he made his living, but about himself. Sometimes, sitting at a bar and staring at himself in the glass, somewhat dulled and clouded by the indifferent swipe of a bar rag, he failed even to recognize himself. His light brown hair, further lightened by the sun, seemed to belong to someone else. The pale blue-gray eyes were like small pools that went deep inside a man he didn't know. He could assess himself then almost dispassionately, and came away baffled.

When the cigarette had burned down almost to the nub, he pinched off the glow, watched it drop into the street below, flaring as it fell, then landing without a sound and winking out. Stripping the butt, he clapped his hands free of tobacco and went back to bed, leaving the curtain pulled aside and letting the moonlight spill through the open window.

The next time he woke, it was morning. Red light poured into the room as the sun climbed over the horizon. He lay there watching it turn orange then yellow. Off in the distance, he could hear the insistent chirp of early birds, and the clop of hooves on the dusty ground.

Monroe came awake slowly as he lay there, not wanting to sleep but not yet wanting to get up. For a moment he imagined what it would be like if he were to walk to the livery stable, climb on his horse and ride away, not just from Monroe and its jail and the waiting prisoner, but from his job, from his life, and from who he was.

But if he left himself behind, he wondered, who would it be on the big roan? Who would climb down from his saddle in the next town, the next territory, the next life?

It was tempting, but only for a moment. He was what he was, just as Barton Rawlings was what *he* was. And he could no more change than gold could become silver. He was fixed as completely and permanently, frozen in time and place as surely as any fly trapped in amber, locked forever inside himself.

Getting to his feet, he thought for a moment about ordering a bath, then realized that there was no point. In an hour he would be back on the trail, and fifteen minutes after that, he would be as dry and dusty as he was at the moment. He settled for washing himself in the small commode, pouring tepid water and using the rough brown soap the hotel provided.

He scraped his whiskers, staring at himself in a small mirror, watching his skin redden under the blade, and it seemed for a moment as if he were creating a face the way a sculptor might, carving what he was from something that was not him, painstakingly slicing away everything that was not Lex Cranshaw and leaving a younger looking but no less ancient man to stare back at him from the oval glass.

When he was ready, he went downstairs and walked to the livery stable. Paying the attendant, he made arrangements to have his horse ready in an hour, and also asked for Rawlings's mount to be saddled, fed, and watered, then walked back to find a restaurant.

He wasn't really hungry, but it would be his last decent meal for a few days. After ordering eggs and ham, he sipped a cup of coffee, sitting with his back to the room and watching the early morning traffic in the street. Finishing his coffee, he saw Lute Olson headed toward him and watched as the sheriff entered the restaurant, spotted him, and smiled.

Taking a chair across from him, Olson said, "Morning, Mister Cranshaw. Sleep well, did you?"

"Not really."

"You mean to say our fair city makes you uncomfortable? Well, city might be overstating the case right now, but"—he shrugged—"you got to start someplace. If I had to guess, I'd say in ten years you wouldn't recognize this town."

"That's probably true. I suppose the railroad will mean a lot of changes around here."

"Oh, you can count on that. We got folks just lining up to buy land, and other folks just itching to sell. Fact is, pretty soon, when the word spreads, the bank'll be near to overflowing. I don't suppose that might have been why your Mister Rawlings was so keen to be working on the railroad, do you?"

"I have no idea, Sheriff. It hardly matters now, though. Besides, he was a small-time bank robber. Never got more than a few hundred dollars."

"Practice makes perfect, Mister Cranshaw. Maybe

that's what he was up to. Whatever, I can't say I'll be sorry to see him leave. Or you either, for that matter. I kind of like Monroe the way it is, nice and quiet. Maybe sleepy's the right word."

"I think you better get used to the idea of change, Sheriff. Once that railroad hooks you into the Santa Fe, things'll change for good."

Olson sighed. He was about to say something else when the waitress appeared with Cranshaw's breakfast.

"Morning, Marybeth," Olson said. "Got any coffee handy?"

"Sure thing, Sheriff. Be right back." She set Lex's meal down on the table then walked back to the kitchen.

"Pretty little thing, ain't she, Cranshaw?"

Lex nodded.

"Ever think about settling down with a little woman like that? Have a couple of kids?"

That was a painful subject, one Lex would not discuss, and the look on his face must have been easy to read because Olson dropped it. "What time you fixin' to leave?" he asked, shifting gears abruptly.

"About an hour. Already made arrangements at the livery stable."

Marybeth was back with an empty cup in one hand and a coffeepot in the other. She refilled Lex's cup then poured one for the sheriff. "Thanks," he said. "Tell Mister Hemmings that Mister Cranshaw's breakfast is on me, would you, Marybeth?"

He sipped his coffee then, barely wincing as he swallowed a mouthful of the steaming hot liquid. "I got a few things to tend to, then I'll wander over to the office. Reckon I'll see you in a bit," he said.

"Yeah, you will."

Olson took another sip of coffee. "That's the only thing I want for breakfast," he said. "Never could stand to work with a full stomach."

"You come to see me for some reason, Sheriff?" Lex asked.

Olson shrugged. "I don't think so. Just trying to be hospitable, is all. Why?"

"Seems like you got something on your mind."

Olson shook his head. "Not really. If I'm annoying you, I can . . ."

"No. You're not annoying me. I just don't quite understand what you're doing here. I don't mean at this table. I mean in Monroe. Seems to me like . . . I don't know what."

"Fact of the matter is, Cranshaw, that I kind of see myself in you. A much younger version, of course. I used to have high hopes, high ideals, whatever you want to call 'em. But time, well, it has a way of taking the starch out of a man's shirt, if you know what I mean. Kind of grinds him down. I guess I was just trying to get close to what I used to think I was."

"Fair enough."

"You be careful, won't you? It'd be best if you just put a bullet in Rawlings and left him out there to rot. I suppose that's what I come to tell you. But I don't guess you'd agree, and I don't guess I'd blame you. Still, it's worth thinkin' about. Make life as simple as you can, Cranshaw, because it has a way of getting awful complicated on its own."

"Thanks, Sheriff, but I have to do it my way."

"No cutting corners, eh?"

Lex shook his head. "Nope."

Olson finished his coffee and stood up. "See you at my office," he said.

LEX WALKED to the livery stable, something chewing at him, something he couldn't put his finger on. The street was quiet. Stopping to glance along its length, he saw horses where horses should be, their tails switching in the early morning sun. He could see the jewel-like glint of flies as they darted around the placid animals, dodging the tails to land, then sailing away whenever one came too close.

Shop doors were open. But the chairs on the boardwalks were empty. There wasn't a soul in sight, as if everyone were hiding from something in the air. He almost stopped, then decided it didn't really matter. In a half hour, Monroe would be behind him, a dusty memory slowly fading until it blurred into the memories of a hundred other dusty towns.

At the livery stable, the owner was sitting in his office, a stack of papers in front of him, his hands folded into a neat pyramid as if to hold the papers against a wind that had not yet arrived.

"I came for my horse and for Rawlings's horse," Lex said.

The liveryman looked at him as if he hadn't understood.

"The horses." Lex said. "Are they ready?"

"Yours is. The big roan, right?"

Lex nodded. "What about Barton Rawlings's mount? The black?"

The liveryman shook his head. "Gone. Somebody already come for it."

"What are you talking about? Who came for it? When?"

With a shrug, the liveryman said, "I don't know who. They said they was friends of Rawlings. The horse was paid for, so I . . ."

"When?"

Spreading his arms wide, the liveryman said, "Hey, what do I know? I don't have a watch. Can't afford one. I just . . ."

And Lex heard the first shot before the man could finish. He wheeled around and sprinted out into the street. He heard another gunshot, its echo muffled. The street was still deserted, and he ran down an alley next to the livery stable to the back. Four men sat on horses at a point that had to be directly behind the sheriff's office.

He started to run as three more men appeared, their horses already at a full gallop. The first four jerked the reins and followed. Three more gunshots, fired more for the intimidation value than any other purpose, cracked as Lex ducked instinctively. He jerked his Colt free and continued forward at a crouch.

The horses were pulling away from him, and he dropped to one knee to fire a shot over the heads of the riders.

One turned, and Lex knew without having to think about it that it was Barton Rawlings. The man's size alone would have been enough, but Rawlings was still wearing the bright red shirt he'd worn the night before.

Rawlings jerked the reins and wheeled his mount in a circle so tight it nearly stumbled. Charging back toward Lex, Rawlings aimed a pistol and squeezed the trigger. The bullet slammed into the shake shingles just over his head, and Lex hit the deck.

There was no cover anywhere close, and as Rawlings thundered down on him, Lex brought up his own revolver and fired once, then rolled against the base of the wall.

Rawlings was grinning from ear to ear, his teeth glittering in the sunlight, his mustache wriggling as his face contorted into a parody of amusement. He fired again, and the bullet passed through the brim of Lex's hat before burying itself in the wall behind him.

Lex lost the grip on his Colt as he tried to scramble away, and there was no time to retrieve it. He reached a corner and ducked around it and out of the line of fire, just ahead of another shot.

Rawlings thundered past, his deep-throated laugh echoing in the alley, sounding disembodied, as if the man himself had vanished, leaving just his scorn behind. Rawlings turned again, galloped past the alley and fired one last shot, narrowly missing Lex before disappearing in a cloud of dust.

Lex sprinted back to the corner in time to see

Rawlings racing after the others who were already at the far end of town. He ran down along behind the buildings, stopped to retrieve his pistol, and dashed to the rear of the sheriff's office. The back door was open, and he ducked inside.

Two men lay on the floor of Olson's office, one bleeding from a gunshot wound of the chest. Every labored breath brought forth a small burst of bloody foam. Lex glanced at the second man and knew, even before he bent to check for a pulse, that the man was dead. A pool of blood had already spread out from under him. Two holes in his back, entry wounds, would be matched, Lex knew, by two larger exit wounds on the man's chest.

He moved into the cell block, not knowing what he might find and half expecting to find Olson himself, but the cell block was empty, the doors to both formerly occupied cells yawning wide open. He heard shouts in the street and opened the front door in time to see Lute Olson leading a handful of men at a dead run down the center of the street. One of them, seeing the door open, cut loose with a shotgun, and scattered double-ought buckshot across the front of the sheriff's office, taking out the large plate-glass window.

Lex ducked away, turning and covering his neck with his hands as the glass cascaded to the floor with a loud crash.

"Hold your fire," Lex shouted. "It's me, Cranshaw. . . ."

He heard Olson shouting, then the sheriff's drawl directed at him. "You all right, Cranshaw?"

"I'm fine," Lex answered. "Just tell those damned fools to hold their fire."

"Anybody in there with you?"

"Yeah. Two men. One's dead, the other's hurt real bad. You better fetch a doctor. He's got a chest wound and one lung's been punctured."

"I'm comin' in, Cranshaw."

"Come ahead."

Lex heard a rush of footsteps, then boots thumping on the boardwalk. A moment later, Olson stuck his head in through the open door. "Jesus Christ!" Olson shouted. "Danny, you all right?"

Instinctively, Lex glanced at the badly wounded man, whose eyes were open, his head turned toward the sheriff. His lips moved, but he was unable to utter a sound. For a moment, there was only the terrible gurgle as he tried to breathe.

Olson bent over the man, snatched a handkerchief from his pocket, and looked up as three men tried to shuffle inside. "Pete," he barked, "you run and get Doc Hardiman. Tell him double quick. Tell him Danny Tackett's got a sucking chest wound, and there ain't no time to waste."

Then, turning to Lex, he asked, "What the hell happened here?"

Lex shrugged his shoulders. "Your guess is as good as mine, Sheriff."

"I don't want guesses, damn it! I want to know what happened. Now, you gonna tell me, or ain't you?"

Lex let out his breath in an exasperated puff. "After you left the restaurant, I finished my breakfast. I thought you were coming to your office, so I went to the livery stable to get my mount and a horse for Rawlings. But when I asked for Rawlings's horse, the livery man told me it had already been taken. I figured maybe you had come for it, but then I heard a gunshot. I started down this way from the back. Four men on horseback were waiting outside the back of your office. Then Rawlings and two others came out. I don't know any more than that."

"You get a look at any of 'em?"

"Not a good one. They were too far away. Rawlings came gunning for me, but he's the only one I saw clearly. When I got here, I found one man dead and the other bleeding and barely alive."

"We heard the shots, too. I was already on the way here," Olson said. "I had just stopped off at The Wet Whistle to get a couple of men. I wanted to have a few extra guns on hand. Seems like there was a rumor that Rawlings was gonna make a break for it. So . . . well, anyhow, it looks like it was more than a rumor."

Lex nodded slowly. "Yeah, it does at that."

"You see which way they went?"

"East. Probably back toward the T and W work camp. I expect that's where the help came from."

"You're probably right, Cranshaw. But I'll tell you one thing. This ain't just no Ranger matter now. Not anymore. This is personal now. I'm going after Rawlings and if I get him, I'm gonna tear him up. You can have what's left, or leave it for the buzzards. And if you have a problem with that, tell me now, because I'll lock you up and toss the goddamned key down the nearest well."

Lex shook his head. "No, I have no problem with

that, Sheriff. But if we're gonna take him, we better
get a move on. They were hightailing it. And whatever else Barton Rawlings is, he's no fool. He might
have headed toward the camp just to throw us off."

"Don't you think I know that?" Olson snapped. "I
ain't worn a badge for fifteen years without learning a
few things, damn it."

"Looks like you're going to have a chance to show
off what you learned, then, Mister Olson."

"You just stand back and watch me work, Cranshaw. Maybe *you'll* learn something. Come on. We
got to get a posse together."

The sheriff nodded to one of the cowboys standing
in the doorway. "Klaus, you git on down here and
hold this here kerchief. Make sure you keep some
pressure on the hole in Danny's chest."

"Where you goin', Sheriff?" the man addressed as
Klaus asked, stepping into the office and dropping to
one knee alongside the injured Tackett, whose eyes
were now closed. His breathing was still labored, but
the awful suck and wheeze had stopped with the
compression bandage held in place by the sheriff's
thickly veined hand. Klaus pressed his hand over the
back of the sheriff's, then waited for Olson to pull his
away. Klaus then leaned a little forward, keeping his
arm stiff and letting his weight do much of the work.

"Gonna get the man what done this, that's where
I'm goin'," Olson said, getting to his feet.

Without looking at Lex he walked outside, culled a
handful of men from the crowd, which had swollen to
two dozen by now. As Lex eased out onto the boardwalk, Olson was saying, "You boys go on and get
your horses. We ain't got time to pack, so just make

sure you got plenty of ammunition and get your asses back here in five minutes. You ain't here by then, me and Cranshaw won't be here when you do git back."

Turning to Lex, Olson said, "Better run and git your mount, Cranshaw."

Lex nodded, stepped into the street and broke into a sprint. When he reached the livery stable, the owner was already in the street, holding the big roan by the bridle. "Figured you'd be in a hurry," he said, holding the stallion steady as Lex swung up into the saddle. "Your canteen's all filled, too."

"Thanks," Lex said, kicking the roan and driving it toward the sheriff's office.

Olson was already in the saddle by the time Lex rejoined him. Several of the hands were galloping toward the two men, and Olson raised a hand over his head, pointed toward the east end of Monroe and lowered the hand. He didn't bother to wait for the posse members to reach him before kicking his mount into a full gallop. Turning in the saddle, he shouted, "You boys can keep up or get left behind."

THE WORK camp looked strangely peaceful after the assault on the jail and the breakneck ride that followed it. The track had progressed several hundred yards since Lex last had been there. By now, the roadbed had long since passed the graves of Henry Schuster, Thomas Crandall, and Alan Keats. The graves themselves were no longer discernible, the displaced earth long since covered by heavy gravel, the long heavy rails spiked to the cross ties as if someone feared the dead might rise again.

"I reckon we ought to look for that feller Kinkaid," Olson suggested as the posse reined in.

Lex nodded his agreement. "I'll see if I can find him."

He dismounted and approached the lead work crew as the men jockeyed another rail into place. A few yards away, the clang of hammers rang almost musically as another rail was spiked down.

The foreman looked up as Lex approached, and had to cup his ears to hear Lex's question.

"John Kinkaid?" Lex asked.

Still cupping a hand to his ear, the man responded, "What about him?"

"Where is he?" Lex shouted.

The man jerked a thumb over his shoulder. "Back that way. Probably in the main tent."

Thanking the man, Lex waved to the sheriff and hollered that he'd be right back. Olson, as if afraid of being left out of some important discussion, dropped to the ground and shouted, "Wait for me, Cranshaw."

Lex turned and started toward the tent city, moving slowly to give Olson a chance to catch up. The sheriff was puffing a bit when he fell into step beside the Ranger. "Learn anything?" the sheriff asked.

Lex shook his head. "Didn't ask anything important. I think it's best if we keep the gossip to a minimum. The last thing we need is to stir these men up. We'll get a dozen stories and a dozen variations on each. We won't know which way to turn or how far to run."

"In my experience, you can never have too much information," Olson argued.

"That's true, if it's reliable information," Lex agreed. "But a place like this, there's a lot of opinion and very little hard information. It's like the army, that way. You were in the army, weren't you, Sheriff?"

"No I wasn't, sorry to say."

"Don't be sorry. You didn't miss a thing." As they neared the first line of tents, all of which had their sides rolled up to let what little moving air there might happen to be pass through, Lex waved to two men sitting at a small folding table. A deck of cards sat between them like a stone wall, and stud hands curled in front of their faces like fans in the hands of French royalty.

"John Kinkaid?" Lex asked, ducking under the rolled side of the tent.

One of the card players deigned to remove one hand from his cards just long enough to stab it toward the large tent two rows away, then dart it back to regain control of his cards. "Over there," he said.

Olson chuckled. "Never seen a hummingbird could move that fast, did you? I expect that must be a royal flush he's got there."

Lex laughed. "At least."

The two lawmen moved on through the next row of tents, then turned left toward the largest of the tents in the next row. Unlike the others, this one did not have its sides rolled against the heat. Lex led the way to the entrance, ducked under the flap, which was doubled into a thick triangle and tied in place with a heavy cord.

"Mister Kinkaid," he called.

"Who is that? Who's there?" As Lex ducked down low enough to see the railroad foreman, he saw Kinkaid sitting at a table, what appeared to be survey maps spread out in front of him. He was peering at the entrance, his eyes narrowed to slits. Reaching into his pocket, Kinkaid took out a pair of spectacles, laboriously looped them over his ears and then let his features relax. "Mister Cranshaw," he said. "What in the world are you doing here?"

"May I come in? Sheriff Olson is here with me."

"Of course, of course. Come in." He stood up and

stepped around the table, nearly tripping over a heavy paper tube, apparently used to hold the maps, which lay on the floor.

Awkwardly, he shook Lex's hand, then the sheriff's. Turning abruptly, he grabbed a pair of folding canvas chairs and opened them, setting them almost meticulously by the table, adjusting their positions several times until they sat perfectly stable on the ground. "What brings you gentlemen out here? I thought Mister Cranshaw was leaving for Austin."

"There's been a change in plans," Lex said. "Not by choice."

"Has something happened?"

"You bet something's happened," Olson barked. "Two men were killed in my jail, and Barton Rawlings and that other man have busted out. They were headed this way. But they had help, and if I was to guess, I'd guess that help came from right here."

"Oh, I don't think so. I . . ."

"Look, Mister Kinkaid," Olson exploded. "I don't care what you think. Somebody come along and broke Rawlings out of jail. He was working here, so if he has any friends in the area, they were from here, almost as sure as God made little green apples. Now, what we want from you is help. You want to give it or do we have to take it?"

"But . . ."

"No buts, Mister Kinkaid. We don't have a whole lot of time."

Kinkaid looked at Lex, his face somewhere between hurt and bafflement. "Mister Cranshaw, I don't know what I can do."

Lex dropped to one of the chairs, but Olson was in

no mood to sit down. He took a step closer to Kinkaid, appearing to loom over the railroad man, despite the meager difference in their statures.

Lex looked up at Olson. "Give the man a little room, Sheriff, why don't you. It's not like he's done anything wrong."

Olson bobbed his head. "I know that. I do. It's just that I'm"—he stopped to scratch at the back of his neck for a moment—"frustrated, I guess that's what I am. Just so damn frustrated. I didn't take this all seriously enough, and now two men are dead, and I guess I figure it's my fault, somehow."

"That's done with, Sheriff. What we have to do now is decide what our next step ought to be." Turning to the railroad man, Lex asked, "Is there anybody missing from your crew, beside Rawlings and the two men we caught with him?"

"I don't know. It's a big camp, and . . ."

"Think, Mister Kinkaid. You have to think." Olson looked apologetic, but Kinkaid didn't seem to notice.

"It's a large crew. I don't . . . things have been so disorganized the last couple of weeks. The men are angry, they come and go when they feel like it. Some of them have run off. I'm sure of that, but . . ."

"Is there any way you can tell us how many are missing and who they are? You said you had the payroll list. Can you use that somehow?"

Kinkaid shrugged. "Sure, I suppose. I'll have to get all the men together and . . ." He hesitated for a moment, as if uncertain what to say next. "It'll mean stopping work. The railroad won't like that. They're . . ."

"Whatever it takes, Mister Kinkaid, just do it, would you please?" Lex slapped a hand on one thigh to emphasize the seriousness of the request, and Kinkaid gave a start, then blinked in nearsighted embarrassment. Then Lex added, "I don't imagine the railroad very much likes the idea of people shooting up its employees, either."

"Of course," Kinkaid said. "Of course. I'll get them all here as soon as I can. It'll take a while."

"Just hop to it, Mister Kinkaid," Olson said wearily. Then, as an afterthought, he added, "Please?"

Lex watched him go out of the tent. He took a deep breath to calm his nerves. The pungent aroma of creosote was everywhere. It was overly strong but almost pleasant. In the distance, Lex could hear the steady ring of sledgehammers driving spikes, the sound of each blow rising in pitch as if some unseen musician were tightening the tuning keys on his instrument until the last solid blow ended with a dull crack as the last fraction of the metal spike was driven into the wood and there was nothing left to vibrate.

Olson fidgeted nervously, his hands folded behind his back as he walked around the table, picking up things, glancing at them absently and dropping them again without being sure they had registered on his brain.

"You know, Cranshaw," he said, "I guess I owe you an apology."

"No need."

"No, no need, but I feel like I ought to offer it anyhow. If I hadn't been so damn cocksure, maybe I'd have seen this coming. I should have been more cooperative. It just didn't seem like . . . hell, I guess what I'm trying to say is, you spend enough time in a tiny bowl, you get thinkin' you're a big fish. Then you start actin' like one, ever' chance you get. That's what I done to you. I high-hatted you, treated you like you was some snot-nosed kid. And now two men are dead, and it's my fault."

"Don't blame yourself, Sheriff," Lex said. "The fact of the matter is, Rawlings would have been in the same cell on the same night, whether you acted any differently or not. The end result would be the same."

"I could have taken it more seriously. I could have had more than two men on guard. I could have . . ."

"Sheriff, you could have called for the army, but that wasn't necessary. As to the rest, who could have expected things to work out like they have?"

"Oh no, Mister Cranshaw. They ain't worked out. Not yet! But they will be, I can guarantee you that. I make a mess, I clean it up my own self. I made this mess, and I mean to see it through to the end."

"Sheriff, there's no need to put yourself through that sort of wringer. You didn't do anything wrong. What you have to understand about a man like Rawlings is that he's not like you and me. He's not like most criminals. It seems to me like there's a new breed of outlaw roaming around out there. I don't know where they came from, maybe the war. But the days of the gentleman bandit tipping his hat to the ladies are long gone. What we have to deal with now is the kind of man who will not only smile when he cuts your throat, but he'll dip his fingers in the blood and write a message to the lawman. Barton Rawlings is a man like that. Of all the murders he's been involved with, not a one was necessary, and not one was accidental. They were flat out, cold-blooded murders, murders that he committed because he wanted to commit them. If I had to guess, I'd bet that your two men were alive and unharmed until Rawlings got out of his cell. I'd bet it was he who pulled the trigger. There's no way to prove that, of course. But that's what I'd bet."

"Maybe yes, maybe no. But that don't change things. It doesn't bring those men back, and it don't make me feel better. I made a mistake, and they paid for it with their lives, Mister Cranshaw."

"Thinking like that can eat at a man, he isn't careful, Sheriff."

"Yeah, well, I can't help that. Where the hell is that little railroad weasel, anyhow? Time's awastin'."

THE MEN filtered into the tent in twos and threes. Kinkaid stood at the entrance, tallying them as they entered, making marks on a sheet that must have been a work roster or a payroll. That many men, working hard and gathered in close quarters in high heat, soon filled the tent with a stench that was no less unpleasant for all of its honorable origin.

Olson sat glumly at Kinkaid's table, one hand drumming its fingers on the scarred wood as if it were somehow detached and had a life of its own. Lex sat with his arms folded, studying the faces of the men as they stood in small groups and whispered among themselves. He didn't know what he was looking for, but had the feeling that if he were careful enough, he just might manage to find some little clue, some vague hint, that would tell him the one thing he wanted, and desperately needed, to know.

But try as he might, all he saw was a sea of sun-bronzed faces, streaked with sweaty rivulets where perspiration had trickled down over the dust, darkening it and turning it to a dark beige paste. Their eyes were hooded, as if they were afraid of revealing something they didn't know they knew. Their voices were soft, not so much for fear of being overheard, but because they weren't quite sure why they had been summoned so abruptly, and, as always when men are gathered together on short notice, they feared the worst. For soldiers, it was the fear of unexpected combat. For workers, it was the loss of their jobs.

Lex had been there, part of both groups at one time or another. He knew the tiny fears that scurried around inside their skulls, like hamsters in their wheels, the endless circuit running faster and faster, until the legs gave out and the heart burst, and the twitching corpse of reason gradually lay still.

Finally, as two more men entered, Kinkaid nodded to Lex. "That's all, that's the lot of 'em," he said.

Lex stood up. "How many missing?"

"Nine. I'll write them down. What now?"

"I'd like to speak to the men, if you don't mind."

"Go ahead." Kinkaid tore off a strip of paper and began to transcribe the names of the missing men with the nub of a thick-leaded pencil.

Lex rapped his knuckles on the table to get the attention of the men. The hushed conversation buzzed a little louder for a few moments and men rushed to finish interrupted thoughts, then it died away.

"I suppose you're wondering what's going on here," Lex said. "And I'm going to tell you, but first I want to ask you a few questions. I'd appreciate it if you'd give me straight answers."

One of the workers leaned forward. "I got a question or two for you, mister. Who the hell are you? And why should we tell you anything?"

"Fair enough," Lex said. "My name's Lex Cranshaw. I'm a Texas Ranger. And the man sitting here at the table with me is Sheriff Lute Olson, over from Monroe. I expect some of you have run into him at one time or another. Most likely on a recent payday. But whether you remember him, or Monroe for that matter, is beside the point."

The men laughed, and Lex realized he had gotten off well. Now, if only he could hold their attention long enough to convince them to trust him. When the laughter subsided, Lex looked at them in silence for a moment. "Most of you, if not all of you, were here the other day when Henry Schuster, Thomas Crandall and Alan Keats were murdered. And if you *were* here, then you know that the three men responsible for those murders were run down, one of them killed, and the other two, Barton Rawlings and a man whose name we don't know, were arrested and taken to Monroe to jail."

"Tell us something we don't know, then," one of the men shouted.

Lex glared at the man. "All right, I will. This morning, Barton Rawlings and his unidentified sidekick escaped from jail. They had help, at least five men and possibly more. In the process, two men were killed. You also may not know that Barton Rawlings was already wanted for at least three murders before he ever started to work for the T and W."

"What do you want from us, Cranshaw? You had

him once, and you let him get away. There ain't much we can do about that."

"What I want from you is your cooperation. I have the feeling some of you may have some idea where Rawlings is headed. You might even know where he is right now. I'm not suggesting that any of you have guilty knowledge, that you're in cahoots with him. But he may have said something, anything at all, something that might not have meant anything to you at the time but might make sense now."

"Bart never did talk much."

"Maybe not, but he worked with you for weeks, maybe months . . ."

"Three months," Kinkaid put in, standing on tiptoe to make himself visible to Lex. "Exactly three months."

"All right, three months, then. Thank you, Mister Kinkaid. Now, three months is not a lifetime, but it's a long time. Especially out here. There isn't a hell of a lot to do here once the sun goes down, except sleep, play cards . . . and talk. During that three months, I'm betting that one or two of you must have had a conversation, no matter how short and how seemingly inconsequential, with Barton Rawlings. If that's true, then I'd like to talk to you about those conversations. I'd also like to know whether or not any of the men who are absent, according to Mister Kinkaid's tally sheet, were friendly with Barton Rawlings. Mister Kinkaid, can you read those names for me, please?"

Kinkaid nodded. He cleared his throat, then moved forward a couple of steps. "Matthew O'Loughlin . . . Peter Halliday . . . Patrick Walsh

. . . Steven Jennings . . . Michael Brady . . . Patrick Brady . . . they were brothers, Mister Cranshaw . . . Walter Oberst . . . Sven Nater . . . Harris Bradley. That's the lot of them."

"Thank you, Mister Kinkaid. Now, did any of you ever see any of those men with Barton Rawlings? More often than you saw Rawlings with anyone else?"

There was a long pause. Feet shifted on the dirt floor of the tent, and Lex heard a few throats cleared, as if one or more of the men were debating whether or not to respond and, if so, how.

"I want you to understand that Rawlings is a very dangerous man. I also want you to realize that if you choose not to talk to me, there is nothing I can do about it. But you are all working men. You probably have families, most of you anyway, people who depend on you. The same is true of most of the men Barton Rawlings killed. These were innocent men, men who had jobs because they had to work, men who had families who needed them, who relied on them, who cared about them. Put yourself in the position of those men, and think what it must be like for their families now. Think what it would be like for *your* families, if somebody came along and snuffed out your life with about as much care as a man spitting into a cuspidor. It seems to me like human life ought to be accorded more respect than that, that decent men deserve better than that."

"What's in it for us?" the same workman demanded. "You can talk all you want, but we've been breaking our backs here for months. We don't get paid when we're supposed to. Some of us would walk out of here in a minute, but we can't afford to leave because the company owes us too much money. Three or four months of work. How are we supposed to live, families or not? We're tired of it, tired of being abused. Maybe not everybody here will say it, but *I'll* say it. Bart said it, and then he did something about it. As far as I'm concerned, that's worth something. You talk about the other killings. Those are just words. Words that don't mean anything. I can't eat words, no matter how long I chew on 'em. But I don't give a damn about Henry Schuster or Tom Crandall. I have to look out for myself, first."

Lex listened quietly, studying the other faces, many of which wore the same angry expression, had the same clenched jaw beneath them. He knew what the men were angry about, and part of him even sympathized with that anger and, more particularly, with the sense of impotence that was both a part of and a source of that rage.

"I understand . . ." he said, but the man cut him off.

"We don't care whether you understand. You come here asking for our help, but I'm here to tell you you ain't getting no help from me. None."

"All right," Lex said. "But I hope you'll think about what I've just said. The sheriff and I will be here for another thirty minutes or so, if any of you have anything you want to tell us."

Without waiting to be told, the angry workers started to leave the tent. As they ducked under the flap and out into the sun, their voices rose. The discontented mutter of a few moments before turned into heated dispute, and before the last man was out

of the tent, a fight had broken out. Lex and the sheriff
pushed through the stragglers and out into the hot
sun.

The combatants had squared off, and several men
had formed a circle, egging them on. Lex recognized
one of the fighters as the man who had argued so
forcefully with him. Olson, disgusted, shoved his way
into the middle of the circle, but the two men at its
center paid him no attention.

"Come on, break it up, there," Olson barked.

The men continued to circle, each looking for an
advantage, sometimes glancing at the ring that sur-
rounded him, as if looking for an ally. "Go on,
Tommy, bust his head open," somebody said and, as
if in response, the arguer charged his opponent, driving a shoulder into his midsection and landing a vi-
cious hook to the ribs at the same time. The charge
carried both men to the ground, where they rolled
over once, then again, as they tried to gain the upper
hand.

"Break his fucking neck, Paddy," another of the
onlookers shouted. "Gouge him, gouge him."

Olson jerked his pistol from its holster and
thumbed back the hammer. For one crazy moment,
Lex thought the sheriff was going to shoot one or
both of the fighters, but he aimed at the sky and
squeezed the trigger.

The sharp report seemed to freeze time. Both
boxers turned to look up at the sheriff, who bobbed
his head angrily. "I said to quit it, you sons of bitches.
And I meant *quit* it. Get up."

He reached down to grab the arguer by the collar
and started to haul him away from his opponent. The

man's shirt gave with a shriek, and the sheriff stared for a moment at the ragged patch of faded denim in his hand, then threw it to the ground in disgust.

"You're like a pack of wild dogs, you are," Olson snapped. He reached out again, this time grabbing the man on top by the biceps, and dragged him away. The man on the bottom, reluctant to pass up an advantage, no matter how fleeting, lashed out with a foot and caught his opponent in the groin, then rolled to one side as the man who had been kicked doubled over and collapsed with his hands clutching his crotch, then lay there shuddering, one long moan escaping before he retched.

Glaring at the onlookers, Olson thumbed the hammer back once more. "Now, I'm gonna count to five," he said. "And I promise you that I will shoot the nearest man as soon as I do. Get the hell out of here. Now! One . . . two . . ."

The men started to scatter, breaking into reluctant runs that picked up speed as Olson barked ". . . three . . . four . . ."

By the time the sheriff reached five, the only man left was the crumpled figure on the ground. Olson prodded him with a boot, provoking a groan. "Get up, you dim-witted horse's ass. Get to your god-damned feet or I swear to God I will put you out of your misery right now."

He rolled over and sat up, then doubled over. "Son of a bitch shouldn't have done that," he groaned.

"You asked for it," Lex said. He squatted beside the man and patted him on the shoulder. "You'll be all right."

The man looked at him almost disbelieving, the way only a man in intense pain can look at someone who assures him there is light at the end of the tunnel. He took a deep breath then, and reached out to rest one hand on Lex's knee.

"Maybe you're right," he said. "Maybe I got it all wrong."

"If you know anything," Olson said, "now's the time to tell us."

The man nodded, swallowed hard, and said, "Maybe you're right."

"Let's have it, then," the sheriff snapped.

"That fella with Rawlings, the little one looked like him, that was his half-brother, Martin."

"You hear them talking? You have any idea what Rawlings is up to?"

The man shook his head. "No. But I know a couple of those names Kinkaid read off. They were friendly with Rawlings. Not real friendly. But some. I guess they must have been the ones helped him bust out of jail."

"Who are they?"

"Let me get my wind back," he said. "Soon as I can talk without tearing my guts open, I'll tell you what I know."

"MISTER KINKAID," Lex said, "I think I know what Rawlings is planning to do."

The railroad man stood with a blank expression on his face, but Lute Olson was more direct. "And are you reading the man's mind now, Mister Cranshaw? Are you some kind of medicine show mentalist, is that it?"

Lex shook his head. "Not at all. It's so damned simple I don't know why we didn't think of it sooner."

"Don't you be dragooning me into your hare-brained schemes," Olson insisted. "I don't have the least idea what a man like Barton Rawlings might be thinkin'. I'm not even sure he thinks at all, so much as acts like some kind of wild animal, doin' whatever occurs to him without any thought whatsoever."

"You're wrong, Sheriff. I know it, and I know what he's planning. I'm sure of it."

"Well, then, are you going to share this great discovery of yours with those of us less inclined to peer into a man's skull and read the wiggles on his brain? Or are you going to take care of it all by yourself?"

Lex smiled distantly. Turning to Kinkaid, whose jaw was still slack in its lack of comprehension, he asked, "When is the train carrying the payroll due here?"

"I don't see what that . . ." Kinkaid started. But then, as the meaning of the question dawned as a distant glimmer, he nodded. "Yes, yes I do see. Two days, give or take."

"Can you find out for sure? Quickly?"

"I can send a wire. The nearest telegraph is still twenty-five miles behind us, or thereabouts. They're using the same right of way, but they're a bit behind."

"Do it," Lex snapped.

"You think Rawlings plans to hold up the train, is that it, Cranshaw?" Olson asked, intrigued in spite of himself. His initial skepticism seemed to have been pushed aside. He leaned across the table, stretching his arms out as if he meant to grab hold of some invisible fact that lay there somewhere on the scarred wood. His hands groped like hungry spiders as their fingers squirmed and wriggled.

"That's exactly what I think."

But Olson wasn't quite ready to accede yet. "Do you mind telling us why?"

"It's the only thing that makes sense."

"How do you figure that?"

"Simple. The men haven't been paid in a long time. They know the payroll is coming. The men who left with Rawlings, who helped him break out of your jail, were close to him, at least as close as he allowed anyone to be. Like him, they were angry about not having been paid. That's, after all, what the argument with Schuster was all about. It's what got Schuster killed. Crandall, too. Keats just happened to get in the way, I think. Rawlings didn't give a damn about Keats.''

''Then why did he run the other way, if he's so all-fired hot to hold up the train?''

''The first time?''

''Hell, yes, the first time,'' Olson insisted.

''Maybe to throw us off the trail. Maybe he thought he could shake us and double back. Maybe he thought he needed more help than he had. Maybe he wanted to throw suspicion in some other direction. If we thought he was in New Mexico, we wouldn't suspect him of having anything to do with the train robbery.''

''And he'd be right,'' Olson said. ''In fact, he's still right. I don't see why you're so damn sure about it now.''

''I'm not sure, but I don't have anything else to go on. It seems to me like we have two choices—we can just try to track him, hope to run him down in two or three days, or we can outsmart him. Let him come to us. He won't be expecting that, and his guard will be down. It'll make it a whole lot easier.''

''I don't know . . .''

''What have we got to lose? If you want, we can play it both ways. You can send a small posse after him, just in case he's waiting for pursuit. That'll get him to lower his guard a little. But we can cover the train, too.''

"For Christ's sake, man, there's hundreds of miles of track out there. How do we know where to look for him? How do we know where to set the trap?"

"First, Kinkaid wires back to have the guard on the train strengthened. Second, we try to figure out the most logical place for him to hit the train. There must be maps from the survey of the right of way. And my guess is it'll be someplace he's familiar with, someplace where he worked while on the crew, so he'll know it cold."

Kinkaid nodded. "That makes sense, actually. One of the men who is missing, Patrick Brady, worked the survey crew. He knows the route as well as anyone on the crew, maybe even better."

"So," Olson persisted, "what you're telling me is that you think Rawlings and his pack of cutthroats are sitting out there somewhere just waiting for that train to come along."

"Why not? They know it's coming. They know it's supposed to be carrying the payroll, and they have nothing to lose and everything to gain by trying to get their hands on it. How much money is there likely to be, Kinkaid?" Lex asked.

Kinkaid shrugged. "I don't know for sure. If it's the full amount, thirty or forty thousand dollars. Maybe less, maybe more. It depends on how much Mister Scott has been able to raise."

Olson whistled. "That's a lot of money."

"You bet it is," Lex agreed. "And it's a lot of bait. I think we'll be making a big mistake if we ignore the possibility that robbing that train is exactly what Rawlings has on his mind."

Olson sucked on a tooth, nodding his head as if

he'd already made up his mind, but his agreement was slow in coming. Finally, just when Lex was about to push him a little, the sheriff said, "Fine, Cranshaw, fine. I reckon it's worth a gamble, all right."

"What do you want me to do?" Kinkaid asked.

"Wire your headquarters," Lex told him. "Find out when the train is expected here. Tell them to add some additional security on the train itself, if it's not too late to do it. Don't tell them why, though."

"Why not?"

"It's possible Rawlings might have someone on the inside. If we tip our hand, we'll lose him and he still might get the payroll. I'd rather play it as close to the vest as we can."

"How do I explain the request for extra guards, then," Kinkaid demanded.

"Just say there are rumors afloat. Make it as tame as you can. They might not even listen, but on the off chance that they do, then it's worth the trouble."

"All right, I'll send someone right away."

Lex shook his head. "Unh, unh. Go yourself. You don't have any idea who might be in Rawlings's pocket. There might be a dozen men out there on his side. Even if there aren't, one of them might see a chance to get on Rawlings's good side and make some money into the bargain."

"Anything else I can do?"

"Get us somebody on the survey crew, somebody who knows the terrain itself, as well as the maps. Make it somebody you can spare. And somebody you trust. We'll need the maps, too. I'm not going to tell him anything here in camp, it's too risky. I'll wait till we get on the trail."

"The trail to where?"

"I don't know yet. Once we're away from camp, we'll let him tell us."

Kinkaid shook his head, as if he'd just listened to the grandest folly one could imagine, but Olson seemed to be convinced, and he slapped the table with an open palm. "By God, Cranshaw," he said, "you just might be on to something here. I sure as hell hope so, anyhow."

Finally, Kinkaid seemed to fall into place. "Why don't you and your men go to the mess tent and get something to eat, while I try to figure out who would be best to send along with you. You're not in a great hurry now, are you?"

Lex shook his head. "No, we're not, but we don't want to look too unconcerned, either. It just might start somebody thinking, and that's something I'd rather not happen."

"Suit yourself. But you can tell them to hurry and eat. It'll be a long ride, no matter what. Unless Rawlings is going to make his grab for the payroll in the middle of open country, you're looking at at least a fifty-mile ride, and possibly more. For all I know, the train has already passed that point, although I don't think so. In any case, we'll know in a few hours. You might as well go with me to Wilson's Gap, which is about where the wire starts."

"Good enough, Mister Kinkaid."

Lex led the way out of the tent, with Olson in trail. It seemed as if the sheriff was now content to take a backup role, as if he had ceded command to Lex without having made a formal concession. That was fine with Lex and, apparently, with Olson himself.

At the mess tent, the members of the posse sat at a long table. Lex grabbed Olson and made him sit at a separate table. When they were seated, Olson complained. "You're making me look like I think I'm better'n they are, Cranshaw," he said.

"Look, Sheriff, I can't tell you your business, and I sure as hell can't tell you how to run your own posse. But you and I both know that we can't afford a slip of the lip here. Until we get away from this camp, there is always the possibility that somebody will say something he shouldn't. The only way to make certain that doesn't happen is to make sure that nobody but you and I know what we're planning. Now, if that makes you look bad, I'm sorry. But the men will understand once we get on the trail and we fill them in."

"Fair enough. I knew you had a reason, but I just . . ."

"You're a democrat, Sheriff. Nothing wrong with that. We should all be like that. But the law makes tyrants of the lawmen. You know that as well as I do. The problem with treating everybody equally is that you leave yourself wide open for abuse from somebody who thinks he's a little better than everybody else, and you give him a chance to do something he shouldn't."

"Maybe you can put it that way. Me, I look at things kinda simple like. I like people and I respect 'em. As long as they respect the law and each other, then I don't give a damn what they do. It's nice to sit down with folks you know and have a beer once in a while, even if you both know that one Saturday night you're gonna have to grab that same damn fool by the scruff of the neck and haul him off to jail because he had a few too many beers with a few too many friends. But that's all right, because you both know there wasn't nothing personal. That's the kind of law I can understand. That's the way I do it, and that's the way I *like* to do it. But you're way out of my league with this Rawlings character, Mister Cranshaw.''

"Not as far as you think, Lute. It's a question of degree. Sometimes I look at the law and think it's like the land itself, like there's always something scraping it away, a little bit at a time, the way the wind and the rain can take good land and turn it into wasteland before you even realize anything was happening. There always seems to be somebody out there like Rawlings. Maybe he's trying something that isn't against the law, but it isn't right, either. So either the law changes or he gets away with it. If he gets away with it, then somebody else comes along and tries to take it a little further, and there's somebody in line behind him, and so on. Eventually, you get to a man like Rawlings, and as far as he's concerned, there *is* no law. He can do whatever he damn pleases, and anybody who tries to put a halter on him ends up in a pine box.''

"Sounds like there ain't no future in the law, Cranshaw. Not the way you look at it, anyhow. Makes me glad I'm a old man.''

"Makes me hope I live to be one, Sheriff.''

LEX SWUNG into the saddle. Lute Olson was already mounted. They had a handful of cowboys, of whom Roy Childress was the only one Lex knew, but if Roy was an example of what he had to work with, he wasn't sanguine about the prospect confronting him. The hands meant well, but their idea of a posse was closer to a picnic than to the grueling pursuit of a man like Barton Rawlings.

These were men who were used to firing their guns on two occasions—Saturday night, stumbling out of a saloon with half a month's pay left behind on the bar, and riding behind a herd of cattle that sometimes bolted at a change in the wind, and for which the crack of a Colt seemed like the most terrifying sound in the world.

Shooting a man who was looking back at you over the sights of his own gun was the longest moment in a man's life, one that seemed to last an eternity. It was a time when the muscles in your trigger finger seemed to have a mind of their own, when the time between the decision to squeeze the trigger and the

95

actual release of the hammer might last a year, and just might be the last moment you'd draw a breath. Whether these men were aware of that hard reality was doubtful. But Lex had no choice but to use them if he wanted to bring Barton Rawlings in, and he would do what he had to do.

The survey man, a squirrelly little fellow whose gray hair looked as if it hadn't seen a comb since he'd left school, and whose mustache didn't resemble human hair so much as a lichen clinging tenaciously to a precarious perch, was named Michael O'Hara. His blue eyes were so dark one had the impression they were at the bottom of deep wells, and gave his face a sorrowful cast.

O'Hara's brogue was a yard thick, and Lex wondered how long he'd been in Texas, but was afraid to ask. The last thing he wanted was to have yet another greenhorn hung around his neck. But according to John Kinkaid, O'Hara knew the right of way from New Orleans to head-of-track better than any man alive. "It's like he's got a map inside his skull," Kinkaid had said. It was the only time O'Hara had smiled, and the expression came and went so quickly Lex was uncertain whether he'd actually seen it or merely imagined it.

As O'Hara climbed onto his horse, he looked awkward, and Lex remembered a time he'd seen an eager Easterner get so tangled in the stirrups that when he finally planted his butt in the saddle, he was facing backward. But O'Hara managed, somehow. And they were finally ready.

If the rest of the work crew was curious, there was no evidence. Most of them were back at their jobs.

And the ring of hammers cut through the tang of creosote in the air. Lex nodded, ceding command of the posse back to Lute Olson, despite the sheriff's apparent reluctance, who raised a hand with all the pomp of a man posing for a military statue, then shouted, "Hooooooo, let's ride," as the hand fell forward.

Lex rode beside O'Hara, curious about the man and anxious to pick his brains, but wanted to get some distance between the posse and the camp before telling O'Hara exactly where they were headed and, more to the point, why. They had gone two miles before Lex edged closer.

"You know why you're riding with us, Mister O'Hara?"

The surveyor shook his head. "No, I don't. Mister Kinkaid said it was because I knew the line that I had to be goin' with you, but he didn't tell me no more than that."

"Let me ask you a few questions, if I might."

O'Hara nodded. "Go ahead."

"What we're looking for is someplace on the line, someplace within fifty or seventy-five miles where the line runs through a draw, or where there're steep walls on both sides. Someplace where the terrain around the track gives an advantage to men on horseback."

"You mean someplace where the train has to slow down, and where it might be easy to stop 'er altogether?"

"Exactly."

O'Hara smiled. "You know, Mister Cranshaw, you're thinkin' I'm such a buffoon that I can't figure out what it is you're after. But I'm no fool at all, I'm not. I can guess what it is you have in mind."

"Oh, and what might that be, Mister O'Hara?"

"You might as well call me Mike. Everyone else does. And what you have in mind is that Barton Rawlings wants to get his hands on the payroll shipment."

"What makes you think that?"

"Sure and it makes good sense. He was like the others, angry about not getting paid. From what I understand, he's killed a few people before, robbed banks, and such. He knows that the train is due anytime, and he wants his money."

"I'm afraid he wants more than just *his* money, Mike. He wants *everybody's* money. Yours included."

"Aye, I know that. It's the way of the world, Mister Cranshaw. I've seen it plenty of times. In Ireland, it was the same. You talk to all these bloomin' Micks about the old sod, and they tell you how beautiful it was. How the colleens were fair, and the lakes were deep and blue. They talk about the green hills and the glens full of flowers. But that's now, where it's a hard way to go. What they don't talk about is the cries of babies in the night when there's no food. They don't talk about havin' to dig a grave for your father with your own hands because there's no money to pay the undertaker, and none to pay the priest to get a Mass said. They don't talk about having to break your back seven days a week just to pay the rent on the land that doesn't even grow enough food to feed your family."

"It sounds like you almost sympathize with Rawlings, Mike."

O'Hara shook his head. "No, I don't. I don't sympathize with any man who would kill someone to take what doesn't belong to him. I don't really have any room in me chest for sympathy for anybody at all. Sympathy is not a cash crop in Ireland, Mister Cranshaw. Nor in Texas neither, from what I can see."

"So? What about it? Can you help?"

"Aye. I can help. And I will. I know the place you're lookin' for, and I'll take you there. I'll show you the maps when we stop to eat."

"Does Rawlings know about this place?"

"I'm sure I don't know."

"Thanks, Mike."

"Don't thank me. I'm just lookin' out for meself. Like you say, it's my money on that train, too, you know. And I need it as much as the next man. Maybe more."

Lex nodded that he understood, then nudged the roan with his knees and moved ahead of the rest of the men, to join Lute Olson at the point.

"That little Mick gonna help us any?" Olson asked.

"He says he thinks he knows where Rawlings will make his move."

"Do you trust him?"

"I don't have a choice, Sheriff. He knows the country, and he says there's only one place makes any sense. If we're right about what Rawlings is planning."

"And are we right?"

"We'll find out soon enough, Sheriff. Soon enough."

"Not soon enough for me, Cranshaw. The sooner we put Rawlings away, the sooner I can get back to Monroe. It ain't much, but it's all I know. And all I need. As it is, I'm thinkin' about moving on. Once that railroad goes through, the place'll never be the same. Be kind of a shame to leave it all behind, though. That's where I buried my wife and two baby boys."

"I'm sorry, Sheriff."

"Aww, hell, I'm almost over it now. Been seventeen years come November. Cholera. You know, you meet Easterners from time to time, and they come out here with their heads all full of strange ideas. I don't know where they get them. The newspapers, I guess. And those dime novels. They expect to see a Comanche under every rock and a Kiowa behind every tree. They figger there'll be wall-to-wall redskins and buffalo by the millions. But it ain't like that anymore. If it ever was. And it ain't the injuns you have to worry about, nor the outlaws neither. That ain't what kills you out here."

Lex nodded vaguely. "No, it isn't."

"You know what does kill you?"

"What's that, Sheriff?"

Olson laughed bitterly before responding. "No, it ain't the injuns or the badmen, Cranshaw. It's life. Life kills you. Takes a piece out of your hide every damn day. Dyin' wouldn't be so bad if we didn't have to live until it happened."

Olson looked at the Ranger, and saw that Lex was deep in thought. "You have a family, Cranshaw?"

Lex shook his head. "No, I don't."

"What about your kin? Your mother and father?"

"Dead. A long time. Back in Kentucky. I'm named after Lexington, as a matter of fact. And sometimes I wonder what the hell I'm doing here."

"You're like most of us, prob'ly. One day you look out the window at the farm, you see the barn needs fixing, the fence is fallin' down and you say to yourself 'Why the hell should I bother? I don't even *like* it here.' That's what I done, anyhow. Packed everything I owned in a wagon. A *small* wagon at that. I was farmin' back in Ohio. It was just me and Millie then, so I says, 'Let's go, hon.' She looked at me like I was crazy. 'Go where, Lute?' And I looked right back at her. 'Hell,' I says, 'who cares. Let's just go.' And we did. And I reckon that's what killed her. If'n I hadn't dragged her out here, she'd prob'ly still be alive. God, I miss her."

It was Olson's turn to grow silent. Lex glanced at him, barely seeing him. He was too full of his own thoughts, and of his own loss. He had been married, too. And like Olson, he had lost not just a wife, but a child. But his scars were more recent. He wondered about the sheriff, wondered whether his own pain would last seventeen years.

But it was rhetorical wonder, really. He already knew the answer. And he knew that he would never stop feeling that pain, not if he lived to be a hundred, turned into some broken-down old man with white hair and a cane, sitting on a front porch somewhere in a rocking chair. And he'd still be thinking about Rosalita when the strength left him, when his feeble old legs could no longer push the rocker, and when his heart gave one last, tiny, hopeless beat before it stopped altogether.

He didn't talk about Rosalita much. Al Hensley, his best friend in the Rangers, knew, but even Al didn't know all the details. They were private knives that cut too deep for anyone to understand, and he learned early on that it was better to keep the pain to himself.

Olson, sensing that he had touched a nerve, tried to change the subject. "I reckon we've gone far enough to treat ourselves to a little rest, don't you think, Lex?"

It was the first time the sheriff had called him by his first name. He knew Olson was feeling bad, and nodded, trying to make his voice sound more cheerful than he felt. "Guess so, Sheriff. Been on the trail for three hours. I suppose we have to worry about Mister O'Hara's tender parts."

Olson grinned. "Don't you worry about that little Mick. Something tells me he's tougher than he looks."

Shielding his eyes from the blazing sun, Olson looked for a likely place to take a break. About a mile ahead, the tops of a few cottonwoods shimmered in the ground heat, and he stabbed a finger toward them. "Don't know if there's water there, but there prob'ly is. I reckon it's as good a place as we'll find. What say?"

Lex nodded. "Fine by me, Sheriff."

"Good. I'll drop back and let them no-accounts know."

MIKE O'HARA spread his maps out on the grass after stamping it flat. Lex and the sheriff knelt, one on either side, as the surveyor smoothed the thick paper with movements so delicate they were almost loving. O'Hara noticed their glances, and said, "If you put as much time and effort into something as I put into these goddamned maps, you'd be careful, too." He smiled, but it was a cold, distant smile, as if he feared they couldn't, or wouldn't, understand what he was trying to tell them.

Then, rubbing a hand across a stubbled jaw, he leaned forward. "Let's see," he mumbled. "Let me find the exact place." He reached out with one finger to brush away an adventurous ant. Rather than crush it on the paper, he swept it away in short strokes, leaving Lex to wonder whether he was being careful of the map or the insect itself. The question was finally answered as the hapless bug reached the edge of the paper, whereupon O'Hara picked it up between his fingers and squashed it.

"Bastard," O'Hara muttered. "Serves you right, it does." Once more he looked at Lex, this time with an embarrassed grin. "There's acid in the ant, you see. If it gets on the paper"—he shrugged—"it could eat through."

"Where are we right now?" Lex asked.

"I was just getting to that," O'Hara answered, without irritation. "I just have to find it." He leaned closer, as if his eyes were failing him, traced a meandering, crosshatched line with the tip of one finger. Then, moving to one side only an inch or so, he nodded. "We're right here . . ."

He snatched a small stone from the roots of the grass and set it down where his finger had been. "See, what I do is, I survey the right of way a few weeks in advance. Then, with India ink, I add the track every night. That keeps it up to date, and we always know what to expect over the next week or two. Lately, though, it doesn't seem to matter as much. We used to order materials far in advance. But now, it seems like the supplies come when Mister Scott can beg, borrow, or steal them, instead of when we need them. That's making the construction cost more, because sometimes we have to sit idle for three or four days at a time when we run out of rail or ties or stone for the rail bed."

He stopped again, and looked at Lex with some embarrassment. "I don't suppose," he said, "all this is of much interest to either of you. You want to know where we can expect an ambush. I just get carried away sometimes. I love my work, and sometimes I forget that I'm all alone in my passion for it."

"What's the scale of this map?" Lex asked.

"What the hell difference does it make?" Olson interrupted. "What's scale, anyhow?"

"One inch equals one mile," O'Hara said. He answered as if Olson hadn't said a thing. It seemed almost as if he sensed some sort of kinship with the Ranger, or at least the presence of someone to whom his business was not all smoke and mystification.

Looking at the pebble and its relationship to the delicate, black crosshatching, Lex said, "So we're about ten or twelve miles south of the rail line, then?"

O'Hara nodded. "That's correct. I can tell you exactly, if you need to know."

"That won't be necessary," Lex said. "I just wanted an approximate idea."

O'Hara traced an imaginary line from the pebble that intersected the rail line another inch or so away. "That's Wilson's Gap," he said. "There's a telegraph station there, and we'll be able to get the information we need as soon as we reach it. I thought it best to go overland, because we save about seven miles by taking the more direct route. I know that you wanted Mister Kinkaid to send the wire, but he felt that someone with some authority had to stay behind to keep things under control."

"That's fine," Olson said. "That's smart. But we'd best get on with the lecture here, or we'll lose whatever time we save just flappin' our gums."

O'Hara looked hurt, but he didn't say anything. Instead, he traced another imaginary line, then plucked a blade of grass, laid it on the line, then trimmed it by pinching it between his fingernails. "This is the most logical place for anyone to try and hold up the train." He spread his palm, splayed the fingers, and set it down over the end of the grass blade. "Almost everything under my hand is an area of rugged hills, winding canyons and rocky draws. In order to save construction time, we followed the indirect route, the way water might. It means more rail had to be laid, but it was better than trying to cut through the hills. That would have taken months of work for a few miles of track."

Placing the tip of his finger over the place O'Hara had indicated almost as soon as the surveyor withdrew his hand, Lex asked, "Why here, Mike?"

"The rail bed winds through a narrow canyon here. The walls are steep, maybe a hundred feet high in some spots. Because it's so narrow, it would be an easy thing to block the train. A few logs might be enough. And if they dynamite the walls, they can block it so completely, they could bury the whole train, if they wanted to."

"And then they'd have to dig it out again, just to get to the money," Olson said. "Sounds like only a damn fool would try that."

"I'm not so sure, Sheriff," Lex argued. "What they could do is block the canyon, a few logs, maybe a few boulders, and then threaten the train crew that they *will* bury the train, unless the money is handed over. Remember, Rawlings has at least seven men, and for all we know, he's got even more than that."

"And if the crew says go to hell, then what?" Olson argued.

"They won't," O'Hara said.

"What makes you so sure of that?" Olson demanded.

"They know how far behind schedule we are already. They know that any further delays might mean the end of the line altogether. The owners of the line can always get more money somehow, or if they can't, they can sell to somebody who already has it. But time is the one thing they can't buy."

Olson didn't seem convinced. "I still ain't sure it's the best place."

"What sort of place would you look for, Sheriff?" Lex asked.

"Someplace open all around. It was me, I'd want to be able to run like the blazes in any direction. I'd ride in, shoot up the train, take the money, and split up right then and there."

"But how do you stop the train?"

Olson shrugged. "Search me. I reckon a few logs'd do it out in the open as well as anyplace else."

"Then we don't have a chance," Lex said. "If Rawlings could hit it anywhere along a couple of hundred miles of track, there's no way for us to cut him off."

"The onliest way I know is to ride like hell and get to that train before he does. Then we can get on board and be there when he hits, no matter where it is."

"But we've already said we're going to suggest they add security to the payroll car," Lex argued.

"Sure. And maybe they'll even listen to you. But if money is as tight as everybody says, maybe they'll cut some corners. Maybe they'll take a chance that Rawlings won't pull it off. Hell, we can't even tell them for sure that we know that's what Rawlings is up to, because we don't know that for certain. We're just spit-tin' in the dark. Maybe we get the spittoon . . . and maybe we get the floor. Since the floor's bigger, I know which way I'd bet."

"There is one other way," Lex suggested.

"What's that?" Olson asked.

"We can have it both ways. You can take some of the men and follow the track until you reach the train. I can take some more and go where Mike suggests. That way we have it covered from both ends."

"And maybe you find him," Olson said. "What then? You said yourself, he's got seven and maybe more. We split in half, we don't have that many."

"That's only a problem on my end. On yours, there's the security already on the train and the extra men you bring along."

"There is one other way," O'Hara said. "We can wire and ask them to commit to the extra security. We tell them exactly why, even though you hadn't wanted to be that open about Rawlings. If they agree, then all we have to do is take them at their word, then go to the canyon and wait, just in case I'm right."

Olson made a noise deep in his throat, then spat into the grass. He looked at Lex, his face poised on the edge of a decision. Then, shaking his head, he said, "Aww, hell. Let's try it your way. I'd as soon sit on my ass in the hot sun as go scramblin' around lookin' for a needle in a haystack, I guess."

O'Hara grinned. "You won't be sorry. Rawlings knows this country pretty well. He hired on back about here," he said, pointing to a place a half inch before the end of the blade of grass, where the canyon lay. "I wish we knew whether he had dynamite with him, but it's too late to find out now. We'll just have to assume he does."

"Knowing Rawlings," Lex said, "you can bank on it. If he's half as smart as I think he is, then he's gonna do exactly what we think. It's the only thing that makes any sense."

"If I'da known all the trouble this damn railroad was gonna cause, I think I'da moved on as soon as I heard about it," Olson said.

O'Hara looked offended. "Without the railroad, Monroe would be a ghost town in ten years, Sheriff," he said, the tone of his voice echoing the wounded feelings evident in his expression. "You know that."

"Sure, I know it, but I reckon it would be a peaceful death. Kinda like fallin' asleep in a rocker and never wakin' up. That's the way I want to go, instead of chasing some crazy man halfway across the State of Texas."

"You may get the chance to die in your sleep, Sheriff," Lex said, "if we play our cards right."

"Maybe so, Cranshaw. But in order to believe that, you got to forget about who's dealin'."

"I take it we're agreed, then," Lex said, getting to his feet.

"We're agreed, all right, but that don't mean we're happy about it," Olson replied. "I guess we might as well climb back in the saddle and hightail it to Wilson's Gap, or whatever the hell that place was called."

"Wilson's Gap, that's right," O'Hara told him. "We can be there in a little more than an hour. The country between here and there is pretty flat."

Olson stood up and looked at the sun through the

interlaced branches of the cottonwoods. "Mighty hot out there in the open," he said. "Mighty hot. An old man like me ought to have his head examined for traipsin' around in this heat." But he smiled as he walked to his horse.

Swinging up into the saddle, he announced, "Come on, you lazy good-for-nothing bastards. Mount up."

The posse members, who were lounging in the shade, grumbled, but they got to their feet, stretched, and mounted their horses. Lex waited while O'Hara carefully rolled his maps, decided they weren't tight enough, and started over again. When he was satisfied, he placed a gum band around the outside of the tight cylinder and shoved it into a leather tube, jammed its top in place, and snapped it closed.

Waving the map tube like a wand, he tapped it against his empty hand. "Not many men can fit their life's work into somethin' this small, Mister Cranshaw," he said. There was just a hint of regret in the words, but Lex let it slide.

Climbing onto the roan, he nodded to O'Hara. "When that railroad is finished, Mike, I think you'll have more than a little to be proud of," he said.

"Maybe. But, as sure as I'm standing here, there won't be a blessed soul ever heard of Michael O'Hara."

14

WILSON'S GAP looked like a gussied-up version of Monroe. Half of the buildings had been painted within the past year, and there were signs of imminent prosperity everyplace Lex looked. Eight or nine saloons lined the main street, and already there was evidence of a building boom. The frames of several buildings under construction stood starkly outlined against the faded blue of the sky. The ring of hammer on nail was a constant undercurrent. The shops were busy, and horses were jammed hard against one another at the hitching rails, several of which showed evidence of having recently been built.

It didn't take long to find the telegraph station, and Lex accompanied Mike O'Hara inside, while Olson shepherded the posse to one of the saloons, promising to ride herd on them and to limit the drinking. The promise had provoked groans of protest from several of the men, but Roy Childress offered to shoot the first man who filled his glass more than twice, and Olson backed him up.

"What do you want me to say, Mister Cranshaw?" O'Hara asked.

"Tell your headquarters about the possible robbery. Tell them to add men to protect the train, if it isn't already too late. See if you can find out when it's expected here. That'll give us some idea of how much time we have."

O'Hara nodded. He scribbled a lengthy message, cut all excess words from it, and showed it to Cranshaw, who nodded his approval. Walking to the telegraph clerk's desk, he handed the message over. "I want to send this immediately," he said. "And I'll wait for a reply."

The clerk read the message over, then glanced at Lex with his eyebrows raised. "Never mind, just send it, would you?" Lex snapped.

"Yes, sir, I surely will." The clerk spun in his chair and started to tap out the message, sending it twice to make sure there was no mistake. He got an acknowledgment of receipt, then leaned back to wait for an answer.

While he waited, Lex walked to the front window and looked out into the street. It was not beyond the realm of possibility, he knew, that Barton Rawlings might be somewhere in Wilson's Gap at that very moment. The town was crowded, and teeming with strangers. Unlike Monroe, Wilson's Gap would pay no attention whatsoever to a strange face, even half a dozen of them. People were drifting in and out of town at all hours alone, in twos and threes and by the dozen.

That was the way of a boomtown. You could go to sleep one night in a sleepy little backwater and wake up the next morning to a hustle and bustle you couldn't have imagined the night before.

But the odds were against Rawlings being anywhere close. If he truly intended to rob the train, the last thing he would want to do was to risk getting spotted, however slight the chance. And the men with him were likely to have a taste for liquor, and liquor almost always meant trouble. Men with mayhem on their minds usually tried to drown whatever fears they might have. That made them loud and ornery. And Rawlings couldn't afford a run-in with the law now, no matter how tame or ordinary. The sensible thing for him to do would be to camp within sight of the rail line, and within a stone's throw of the canyon where the robbery most likely would take place.

Unlike O'Hara, the outlaw couldn't find out when the train was coming. Or could he? On a sudden inspiration, Lex turned around to look at the clerk.

For a moment, he debated whether to ask the question, then decided he had nothing to lose. Walking back to the desk, he leaned over it until the clerk put down his newspaper. "Anybody in here lately to send a wire to Texas and Western?"

The clerk folded his newspaper before answering. "Sure. All the time. It's the fastest way to talk to New Orleans, ain't it?"

"I mean the last couple of days?"

"Not that I . . . well there was one feller. But he just wanted to know when the train was due. I told him I didn't know, so he sent a wire. Said he worked on the engineering crew over to near Monroe. Said he was expecting some equipment. That's about it."

Lex looked at O'Hara. "You know anything about that, Mike?"

O'Hara shook his head. "First I heard of it."

"Schuster or Crandall here in the last week or so, that you know of?"

"Nope. That much I can be sure of. Besides, John Kinkaid usually handles that sort of thing. Pecking order, and all of that, you know."

Lex nodded. "What did this man look like?"

"What man is that?" the clerk asked.

Lex sighed in exasperation. "The man you just told me about. The one who sent the wire to find out about the train. . . ."

The clerk shook his head. "Just a man. Nothing special. Except for his size. He was big, real big."

"His hair, what color was it?"

"Black, I think. Yeah, black. Had a mustache, too. But there wasn't nothing special about him."

"Was he wearing a red shirt?"

The clerk looked at him as if waiting for a rabbit to come out of his pocket. "How'd you know that?"

"Never mind. Did he get an answer?"

"Answer to what?"

"His telegram. Did he get an answer to his telegram? About the train?"

"Yeah. Sure."

"What was it?"

The clerk shrugged. "I don't remember."

"Think, damn you," Lex barked, pounding one fist on the desk top. "Think!"

"Jesus, mister. Take it easy. I send dozens of telegrams every day. You don't expect me to remember them all, do you?"

"No," Lex said. "Just this one."

"What's so special about this one? What's so special about the man, anyhow? Like I said, he was just a man."

"Just a man who's killed at least six people," Lex said. "That I know of. And if you don't remember that goddamned message, the number'll be even higher."

The clerk whistled. "Six men, you say?"

"Yes. Six men."

"Well, maybe I can remember . . . wait. Wait a minute. I probably can find it. The message, I mean. He didn't take it with him, so it's probably in the trash out back. Let me look."

"No, you tell me where it is. You wait here in case we get an answer. Where's the trash?"

"Out back. In a barrel. It's prob'ly messy. People spit on the floor, and all, and I got to sweep up at the end of the day, so it all goes together."

"Never mind that," Lex said. "Come on, Mike." Lex glanced at a door behind the desk. "Can I get outside that way?"

The clerk nodded. Lex slipped around behind the desk, hauling O'Hara with him as he pushed open the door and entered a narrow hallway that smelled of recently cut lumber. There was a door at the end of the hallway, and he shoved it open to step out into the heat and sunlight.

To his left, he saw a barrel, mounded to the brim with dirty sawdust. Corners of paper pages jutted through the top of the mound like grass just beginning to sprout.

Lex grabbed one of the corners and tugged the

paper free. It was a draft of a telegraph that had been sent two days before. He tugged another, and a third and examined both. Neither had to do with the train's arrival, and he set them on the ground. "Mike," he said, "we're gonna have to turn this whole damn thing upside down. Give me a hand, would you?"

O'Hara shook his head, eyeing the trash warily, as if he expected it to harbor some virulent disease. "Sure and it's a mess, ain't it?" he said.

Then, without further comment, he leaned on the rim of the barrel. Lex put his own weight into it, and the barrel tilted over, then fell on its side with a thud. It started to roll, and Lex was forced to run around in front of it to stop it.

Trash had spilled out, and as the barrel rolled, it had laid down a perfectly regular ridge of sawdust, studded with pieces of paper. The stink of the damp sawdust was almost enough to make him gag, but he closed his mouth and nose as best he could and dropped to his knees where he began to retrieve the papers. Shaking each one, he handed it to O'Hara, who skimmed it to see whether it was the one they were looking for.

"You know," O'Hara said, "we *could* just wait inside until we get an answer."

"There's no time to wait. If that train is already rolling, we have to know it. It could be a couple of hours before we get an answer. Maybe even more. Run and get Olson. Tell him to bring a couple of men to give us a hand. I'll keep digging in the meantime."

Holding his nose, O'Hara nodded. "More than happy to get away from the stink of it," he said.

Lex watched him for a moment, then bent to his

work again, snatching at page after page of paper. Most of them were stained with tobacco juice, some to the point of near illegibility, but he couldn't worry about that. If his suspicions were correct, somewhere in the mound of garbage was the answer to his question, an answer that Barton Rawlings might already have received. And he had to know what that answer was.

Page after page revealed nothing. Some were filled with the childlike scrawl of the barely literate. Others were covered with the long, loosely flowing copperplate of someone whose schoolhouse had had more than a single drafty room.

But no matter how delicate the script or how crude the scrawl, he kept on reading. Finally, in a desperation that was close to rage, he upended the barrel altogether, then shoved it aside with his foot. It left a huge mound nearly two feet high, and Lex kicked at it to spread the trash around, looking for that one page he knew had to be there.

He looked up as Lute Olson stepped out of the rear of the telegraph office. The sheriff was followed by Mike O'Hara, Roy Childress, and another of the cowhands.

"Find anything yet?" Mike asked.

Lex shook his head.

"Whew!" Olson spluttered. "What a mess. What the hell are we looking for, anyhow. The Mick, here, was jabberin' so fast I didn't catch half of what he was tryin' to say."

"Somewhere in here is the answer to a telegram that I think Rawlings sent to New Orleans. If I'm right, it'll tell us what time the train arrives. And we want to know whether or not he knows that before we head out to the canyon."

"Why can't we just wait for an answer to O'Hara's telegram?"

"Because it might take too long."

"We could just go, then, and . . . oh, never mind." Olson dropped to a squat and started snatching at the papers still poking out of the mound. "I still don't . . ."

"Here it is!" Lex said, slapping a sheet of paper with the back of his fingers to free it from the damp sawdust. "Listen! 'Train due end-of-track Thursday, eight/seventeen. Payroll on board.' "

"I still don't see what good . . ."

"That's tomorrow," O'Hara said. "That means it's too late to put more security men on board. It had already left New Orleans by the time they got our wire. There's no way they could add guards now."

"And that means it's up to us," Lex said. "If Rawlings is out there, and I'd bet the farm on it, then we have less than twenty-four hours to find him."

LEX STOOD on the rim of the canyon and leaned out over the edge. The tracks were far below, twin bands of polished metal that glinted in the afternoon sunlight here and there, and lay wrapped in shadows in other places, where the canyon snaked across the countryside. Just to his left, at the western end, the walls fell away quickly in a pair of steep slopes. The ground was littered with large boulders, but there was no evidence that anyone had tampered with the track. Not yet.

"How long is this canyon, Mike?" the Ranger asked O'Hara.

"Three-quarters of a mile, almost to the foot. This is the narrowest part, but it never gets much wider than this along its entire length."

"You were right. You couldn't ask for a tighter bottle than this. If Rawlings is going to hit the train, he'd be a damned fool to try anyplace else."

O'Hara smiled. "That's what I told you."

Lex waved to Olson and the posse, sitting their mounts in a tight knot just off the track about a hundred yards from the canyon mouth. Olson waved back, and turned to say something to the men. In response, they dismounted, and tugged the reins to get their horses away from the rail line. Lex watched as they took cover among the boulders, then turned to O'Hara again.

"Now comes the delicate part," he said.

"What's that, Mister Cranshaw?" The Irishman wore a slightly bemused smile, as if Lex dealt in some sort of arcane logic that ordinary men couldn't possibly understand. He seemed to lean forward the least little bit, ready to trap the words as they issued from Lex's mouth, the way a butterfly collector nets prizes on the wing.

"We have to see if we can find where Rawlings and his men are camped. They can't be too far from here. They'd want to be able to see the train before it gets into the canyon, so they're probably somewhere at the other end. Unless they've already blocked the tracks partway through the canyon."

"That's for you to judge, Mister Cranshaw. I can't fathom how a man like that thinks. I'm amazed that you can. I suppose you have to have a little bit of the outlaw in you in order to do your job."

"I don't like to think of it that way, Mike," Lex said, flashing a grin, "but I suppose you're right. Come on, let's go back down and tell Olson what we have to do next."

Lex walked back to the roan and swung up into the saddle, then sat with his hands draped over the pommel while he waited for the surveyor to negotiate the intricacies of the stirrups and mount his own horse. When the Irishman was finally in the saddle, Lex said, "You go first."

"Why's that?" O'Hara asked, somewhat surprised. "You had me follow you up."

"Same reason," Lex said. "You lose control or your horse stumbles, I don't want you taking me with you. It's a long fall. No offense, Mike, but . . ."

"Sure and I understand, Mister Cranshaw. I don't exactly cut a dashing figure in the saddle, now do I?"

Lex laughed out loud. "No, Mike, I'm afraid you don't."

"The only horses I ever saw in Ireland were pulling wagons or plows. And they were no match for these great beasts. It's a wonder anyone can control them. I ride as little as possible, and I always feel that I'm this far"—and here he held up his right hand, thumb, and finger a half inch apart—"from the Last Judgment."

"It's not that bad. At least not on level ground. But a slope like this one is tricky even if you were born in the saddle, which I wasn't."

"Don't underestimate yourself. You sit on that animal as if you were part of him. You look like some great centaur, you do. Only I don't think centaurs wore those funny hats."

Lex smiled. "I suppose not, Mike. But I don't suppose centaurs had to deal with the Texas sun. It was all chasing maidens and frolicking in the grass. And the only bows and arrows you'll see around here will be in the hands of Comanches or Kiowas. We'd better get moving."

"Aye, we'd better at that." O'Hara nudged his horse forward, cajoling it rather than commanding it, and the animal, as if conscious of the reluctance of the man who rode it, seemed unwilling to make the descent.

Lex gave O'Hara plenty of room to avoid making the Irishman nervous. Only when O'Hara was a third of the way down the slope did he urge the big roan into motion. He gave the horse its head, and let it pick its surefooted way down the winding path. To keep from closing on O'Hara, he reined in twice, letting the gap widen a bit before pushing on.

Once on the valley floor, he led the way to the boulders where Olson and the posse were holed up.

"What'd you see, Cranshaw?" Olson asked.

"Not much. It's an ideal place for a holdup, though. I can tell you that. But there was no sign of Rawlings or anyone else. At the mouth of the canyon, the track is still clear. I'm going to have to ride through, just to make sure, though."

"Why don't you ride the rim? It'll be easy enough to see down in from up top."

Lex shook his head. "I'd have to walk it. In some places there seems to be an overhang, not much, but enough to make it necessary to lean out over the rim. I can't risk that from horseback. And a man up top can be spotted from a long distance away. If Rawlings is anywhere close, and I know he has to be, he'll most likely have field glasses. If he realizes we're here, it'll make it a whole lot harder to nab him."

"Want me to ride with you?"

Lex thought about it for a moment before answering. "No, I'll take Roy. I think it's best if you stay here and take charge of the men. Keep them quiet, and if you hear anything, come running."

"If you run into one of them skunks, try and take

him kinda quiet. If we can get the jump on them, it'll be a whole lot better for us.''

Lex nodded. ''Just my thinking,'' he said. ''Come on, Roy, mount up.''

Childress was grinning from ear to ear, like he'd just been appointed general of the army. He sprinted to his horse and climbed up into the saddle, snatched the reins from a scrub oak, and backed his horse out of a cut between two large slabs of red stone. One of the hands, a cowboy Lex knew only as Rex, said, ''Don't go shootin' yourself now, Roy. You already cut a hole in your shoulder and we ain't got a sawbones out here.''

''Go on with yourself,'' Childress said, still grinning. ''You're just jealous, is all.''

Rex nodded. ''Yeah, I'm jealous, all right. It ain't everybody gets a chance to have a big rock crack his skull for him. He don't even have to do nothing. Just stand there, is all.''

Childress didn't condescend to answer the jibe. ''I'm ready, Mister Cranshaw,'' he said.

''If we're not back in an hour,'' Lex said, ''you'd better figure something's up.''

''We'll come get you,'' Olson assured him, ''don't you worry about that.''

Nudging the roan into a walk, Lex led the way back toward the canyon mouth. When he reached the beginning of the slope, he reached into his saddlebags for his binoculars, draped them around his neck and waited for Childress to move in alongside of him. ''Roy,'' he said, ''remember, we're going in to see what we can see. We run into anybody, don't get itchy. I don't want any shooting unless it's in self-defense. If they're here, we want to know it, but we don't want them to know *we're* here. Got it?"

"You bet."

Lex hoisted the field glasses to his eyes and scrutinized the rimrock along both sides of the canyon. There was no hint of anyone. But that, he knew, didn't mean no one was up there.

Easing forward, he followed the tracks, keeping just off the roadbed to give the roan solid footing. He kept watching the rim on the left side, then decided to send Childress to the opposite side of the tracks, from where he would have a better look at the right rim of the canyon.

"You see anything, Roy, you let me know."

Childress nodded eagerly. "Sure will, Mister Cranshaw. I appreciate you lettin' me tag along."

"You aren't tagging along, Roy. You're doing the same thing I am. You have half the responsibility here."

"I understand."

Lex led the way in. It wasn't until the mouth of the canyon was fifty yards behind him that he appreciated just how steep its walls were, and just how confined the space would be if the rails were blocked. And there was no shortage of rock to do the job. Great slabs of stone had fallen from the towering cliffs on either side. Some were too big to be moved, but others could be wrestled into place by a handful of determined men. They would be enough to block the tracks and force the train to stop.

Rock falls had to be common here. So common, in fact, that the train crew would probably not even be sure the rocks had been placed deliberately, and they just might make the mistake of getting out of the train without realizing they were moving under the guns of men determined to take the payroll.

The sound of hooves echoed off the walls, multiplying every hoofbeat a dozen times over then multiplying each echo and filling the canyon with the thunder of a ghostly cavalry. Lex was getting antsy, and he didn't know why. He felt the hair stand up on the back of his neck, and it was a warning he could not afford to ignore.

He kept looking up at the rim, expecting any moment to see a hat brim retreat, or see the flash of sunlight on a rifle barrel. But for all his looking, he had nothing but his nerves to rely on. Childress was lagging back a bit, letting Lex take the point, and staring up at the rim in a wide-eyed trance.

They were two hundred yards into the canyon now and, if anything, the walls were higher, and the overhang seemed a little more precipitous. Lex reined in, unable to ignore the prickling nerves any longer. He dismounted and crossed the tracks, tugging the roan behind him.

"What are you doing, Mister Cranshaw?" Roy asked.

Holding a finger to his lips, he whispered, "You stay here, Roy. I'm going ahead on foot. I've got a feeling we're not the only ones in this canyon."

"Don't see no sign of nobody," Childress responded. "What makes you think . . ."

Lex shook his head, once more pressing a finger to his lips. "Tell you later," he said, shaping the words but not sounding them.

Yanking his Winchester from the saddle boot, he

moved over against the wall and started ahead, keeping as close to the rock face as he could manage. The going was rough. He had either to go around slabs of fallen rock, getting closer to the center of the canyon, or to go over them, making his progress painfully slow but cutting down on the risk of exposure. He chose the latter course.

He'd gone another hundred yards, when he heard the crack of one stone against another. Because of the echoing walls, he couldn't tell where it had come from, not even whether it was on the canyon floor or from somewhere up above, perhaps even on the rimrock. Freezing in place, he strained his ears, hoping for a repeat of the sound. But nothing came. The canyon was dead silent.

Once more, he inched forward, starting up the canted face of a fallen slab of stone the size of a front porch. Precariously balanced on top, he paused to listen once more. And again, he heard the crack of stone on stone. This time fainter. Listening intently, he tried again to place the source, but again there was no repetition.

Then he heard something else. And he knew he wasn't alone in the canyon. It was a human voice, too distant for the words to be made out, but unmistakable.

16

EX LISTENED for a moment longer, trying to hear what was being said. He still wasn't sure where the speaker was, but he knew one thing—unless the man was talking to himself, there had to be at least two men. He climbed on over the slab of stone and dropped into a crevice between it and a large, rounded boulder.

He stayed absolutely still for five minutes. He never heard another word. Easing out of the crevice, he slipped along the wall unobstructed for fifteen or twenty yards, to where another stone slab lay cantilevered out over a thick, squat boulder. Dropping to the ground, he crept under the overhanging slab. The canyon bent to the right a few yards ahead.

Rolling to his left to try to see around the bend in the wall, he was able to see only part of the track where it curved to the right. Lex slipped out from under the overhang and got to his knees. He balanced the Winchester, one hand curled through the lever and a finger on the trigger. Glancing up at the rim he thought for a second that he saw the silhouette of a man leaning out, but as his eyes adjusted to the glare, he was able to see that the dark shape was nothing more than a chunk of rock laying on the edge and ready to topple.

Straightening, he moved back toward the wall and pressed himself flat, inching ahead until he reached the bend. The canyon ran straight for nearly a hundred and fifty yards, and he saw two men on foot just disappearing around the next bend. Waiting until they were out of sight, he moved out to the track and stopped for a moment.

His eye caught a wisp of gray smoke, and he sprinted toward it. A cigarette lay on the ground, all but ash, the last eighth of an inch of damp tobacco and paper sputtering before winking out and sending one last curl of smoke, thicker than the previous wisp, up toward the rimrock. He watched it rise until it dissipated. The ground was covered with footprints, obviously left behind by the two men he'd seen.

What had they wanted? he wondered. Why had they stopped here? Scrutinizing the wall, he looked for something that might have drawn them. At first glance, the ground here was no different from the terrain he had already covered on his way through the canyon. There were rocks, of course, the great red slabs and the rounded boulders, but every yard of the canyon was littered with similar stones, large and small.

Moving closer to the wall, he looked up, thinking perhaps the reason lay higher up. But he saw nothing unusual. Looking at the ground again, he noticed that some of the footprints were deeper than the rest, as if the man who made them had been carrying a burden. But if that were so, they should have been deep all the way in, if he had brought something with him, or all the way out, if he had taken something away.

But there was no evidence of either. He looked at the prints again, squatting to feel them with his fingertips. There was no doubt in his mind that they were deeper. But why?

Instinctively, he looked up again. The face of the canyon wall above him was as featureless as every other stretch on either side of it—chunks of rock, weeds, farther up the gnarled trunk of a small tree, its roots twisted like an arthritic claw where it clung to the rock face.

Once more, he looked at the ground, then up at the wall. Changing his angle, perhaps to spot something hidden from where he stood, he still saw nothing out of the ordinary. But there had to be something. Then it dawned on him why the prints were deeper at this spot: one of the men had hoisted the other. That had to be it. The added weight would have deepened the prints of the man on the ground. But what were they doing?

He peered more closely at the wall, conscious that time was slipping away, knowing that the men might return at any moment. And still he saw nothing unusual. Setting the Winchester on its butt and leaning it against the wall, he tried to haul himself up but the only handhold he could find broke off as soon as he put his weight on it. The stone was brittle from weathering, and seemed ready to crumble at the slightest pressure.

He needed help. Unwilling to risk calling to Childress, he had no choice but to go back and get him. Grabbing the Winchester, he sprinted back around the bend. Childress had taken cover among some boulders, and Lex almost missed him. At least the man was thinking.

When he spotted Lex, Childress came out from cover. "What's going on?" he whispered.

"I'm not sure. I think I found something but don't know what it is. I need your help to make sure."

"You got it," Childress said. "Let's go."

Childress started to move past him, but Lex caught him by the arm. "Listen, Roy. You'll have to keep your ears open. There were two men back there. They went back the way they came, but they might be coming back. If you hear anything, just stay calm. We don't want to get into a shoot-out with them. It's best if they don't know we're here."

"I understand. Don't worry about me, Mister Cranshaw."

They went back the way Lex had come, keeping to single file and staying close to the wall. When they reached the spot where Lex had found the footprints, Lex pointed them out. "I want you to boost me up the wall a way," he said. "Just make a stirrup of your hands and I'll do the rest."

Childress nodded that he understood. Placing his back against the wall, he made ready. Lex put one foot in the cupped hands and Childress grunted as he lifted. Lex tried to use his hands to take some of the weight off the cowboy. Teetering, he saw something that looked out of place, a root, or a tendril from a dead vine. But there was nothing else growing in that part of the canyon wall. He reached for it, caught it between his fingertips, and pulled. A couple of rocks came away, one bouncing off his chest and hitting Roy on his wounded shoulder.

The impact caused Roy to lose his grip, and Lex slipped to the ground. "Sorry, Mister Cranshaw. I just couldn't hold on. Let's try it again."

He got himself ready, flexed the wounded shoulder once, then formed a stirrup of his hands once more. Again, Lex vaulted up the wall, then reached out with his left foot to find a small shelf of rock that seemed more solid than the others. Able to take the weight off Roy, this time he was more secure. Once more, he reached for the root and tugged. This time, though, he got more than he bargained for.

Six sticks of dynamite came away from a small crevice in the rock. Lex dropped to the ground and held the lethal package in his hand. "Lookee here," he said.

Childress whistled. "Christ Almighty! Dynamite. Lucky we found it," he said.

"We'll have to put it back," Lex said.

"For God's sake, why?"

"Because we don't know when they planned to detonate it. If they come back and go to set it off, they'll know we've been here."

"But if we leave it, there's nothing to stop them from blowing up the wall and blocking the tracks."

"Yes, there is."

"What? We can't sit here and wait for them and say, 'Sorry, fellas, but we don't think you ought to be playing with dynamite, so . . .'"

"You got any better idea?"

Childress shook his head. "Fact is, no, I don't."

"That's it, then. We have to put it back."

"How 'bout we just put the fuse back, and keep the dynamite? They won't check to see before they set it off. They'd have no reason to."

"But if they light the fuse and nothing happens, they *will* check. And we're right back where we started. No, the only thing we can do is make our plans knowing it's here."

"All right, Mister Cranshaw. You're the lawman. I reckon you know what you're doin'. I sure hope so, anyhow."

Lex smiled. "I don't have any idea what I'm doing, Roy. All I can do is try to outsmart Rawlings. The longer he thinks he's safe, the easier that'll be. But he didn't come this far to walk away empty-handed. He wants that payroll. That's the only thing we know for sure. Let's put the dynamite back and tell the sheriff what we found."

Once more, Childress boosted him up, and Lex replaced the explosives. He had two large rocks tucked in his belt and when the bundle of dynamite was back in its crevice, he placed the rocks over the opening, leaving the fuse sticking out just as it had been when he discovered it.

When he was back on the ground, he started to follow the tracks deeper into the canyon. "Come on, Roy."

"How come you're goin' that way? I thought we were goin' to hook up with Sheriff Olson."

"We will, but first we have to see what else we can find. This might not be the only place they planted explosives. My guess is, there'll be at least one more place. Once they stop the train, they'll want to set another charge, someplace past the end of the train. I know I would.''

"Seems to me like you more or less think just like this Rawlings fella," Roy said, with a grin. "Maybe he's got the right idea. You could make a lot more money his way than yours or mine."

"Maybe so, Roy. But I figure I sleep a whole lot better'n he does," Lex said.

Lex stayed a few yards ahead of Childress, moving from boulder to outcrop to rock chimney. If Rawlings and his men were up ahead, he wanted to be the first one to know it. Childress was enthusiastic, but he didn't think like a lawman. If he ran into someone from the other side, his first instinct would be to go for his gun.

Two sets of boot prints followed the tracks. The men had been making no attempt to conceal their trail, a likely indication that they weren't worried about their presence being known. That could only mean they believed they were alone in the area. And that was all right with Lex.

More than a hundred yards deeper into the canyon Lex found another set of very deep prints. He looked up, trying to spot the second fuse. It took him a few moments, because it was considerably higher up the wall. It was an easier climb here, and the man who had planted the explosives could have climbed all the way to the top, if he had wanted to, once he got a boost from his companion.

The fuse was barely noticeable just sticking out from a crevice in the wall nearly thirty feet off the ground. This time, Lex wasn't going to waste time checking it out. It was enough that he knew it was there. For a moment, he was tempted to push on and see if he could locate the Rawlings camp, but decided against it. There were too many risks and too few rewards.

After checking another fifty yards or so, he stopped in his tracks. "We might as well head back and let the sheriff know what we found," Lex said.

"Don't you want to see if we can find Rawlings?"

Lex shook his head. "No need. We know what he wants and how he plans to get it. Better to make our own plans. We'll have to figure out where to put our men."

Childress looked up at the rimrock. "Up there most likely's the best place."

"You're probably right. But Rawlings might be thinking the same thing. He might have some men on the ground. They can hide in the rocks along here and no one on the train will have a clue that they're there. But he won't take any chances, so I figure he'll have at least two or three men up top. They'll be able to see a long way, and they can cover the whole train from just a couple of positions. He'll probably have one or two men on either side of the canyon. That way, nobody can use the train itself for cover."

"Sounds like you've thought of just about everything, Mister Cranshaw."

"Not everything, Roy."

"What's missing?"

"How the hell we're going to get close enough to stop him. That's what's missing. We can't do it from down here, but if we're up top, we'll have a problem with the men on the canyon floor."

"Have to split up, just like he's prob'ly gonna do, I guess."

"I guess."

17

T WAS near sundown. Lute Olson was still skeptical, but Lex continued to insist that it was necessary to know where Barton Rawlings and his men had made their camp.

"If we know where Rawlings is, we can get the jump on him instead of having to sit here twiddling our thumbs, waiting for him to move. If we have to react, we're giving him an edge that we might not be able to overcome, Sheriff."

"Cranshaw, you try what you're suggesting and you'll most likely end up in a pine box come tomorrow."

"Not if I'm careful."

"Careful ain't enough, Cranshaw. You got to be lucky, too. You lucky, are you?"

"Not so's you'd notice, Sheriff."

"There you are, then. You're taking a big chance. And there ain't much of a payoff. If you were a gamblin' man, I'd like to take you on in a game of faro."

"When this is all over, you're on, Sheriff."

"I can't play cards with a dead man, Cranshaw. But it seems like I can't convince you to stay here, and I sure won't try to hold you against your will. So since you're gonna go, at least take somebody with you."

Lex shook his head. "If I'm wrong, Sheriff, I don't want anybody else to pay for it."

In exasperation, Olson spat into the dust, stomped on the wet spot as if it were a bug, then sighed. "You got to be the hard-headedest sumbitch I ever come across, you know that? What the hell am I jabberin' for? Of course you know that. Well, all right then. But you be damned careful, Lex." Olson clapped him on the shoulder, held on for a moment and dug his fingers into the flesh. "I'm gettin' sort of fond of you," he added, "although only the Lord knows why."

Lex smiled. "I'll be back before sunup," he said, "and we'll talk about it."

The Ranger looped the strap of his binoculars around his neck, tucked a box of shells for the Winchester into his shirt, and pulled the rifle from its boot. Roy Childress hovered at his side. "You sure you don't want me to come along, Mister Cranshaw?"

Lex shook his head. "No thanks, Roy. All I aim to do is get a look at Rawlings's camp. It's got to be close by, and I want to see what we're up against, that's all. We don't even know how many men he has with him."

"You be careful, then."

"I will, Roy. Don't worry about it." Without a backward glance, he started toward the steep slope that led up along the mouth of the canyon. It was a tough climb. The loose rock and soft earth made every step treacherous. By the time he was halfway up, his knees were aching. His shadow stretched for yards ahead of him as the sun dropped close to the horizon. He stopped to look back at the huddled posse, Olson standing with arms akimbo, his hat tilted back on his head, watching as if he expected Lex to change his mind.

The sheriff waved a hand, and Lex returned the wave, then pushed on. He didn't look back again until he reached the tableland up top. The posse was hidden now, as if they wanted to disassociate themselves from his folly. Lex knew they were nervous. And he knew, too, that if anything happened, they wouldn't see it, and they could tell themselves they weren't responsible.

He eyed the sun skeptically, certain that it would vanish before he reached the far end of the canyon. The ground was level, but it was littered with huge rocks, and there was no direct route anywhere but right along the rimrock. Dropping to one knee, he scanned ahead as far as he could see, then checked the opposite rim, just to make sure Rawlings hadn't stationed a man or two across the canyon.

Satisfied that he was alone, he started ahead, keeping three or four yards back from the edge. Here and there, cracks in the ground gave him the giddy feeling that the ledge might give way beneath him, sending him tumbling onto the rocks below. Once, he moved up close to the edge, getting down on his knees and crawling the last few feet, his Winchester left on the ground behind him.

Peering down into the canyon, he swiveled his

head in both directions. All he could see was the rail bed, the polished tops of the tracks picking up the sun's red light and looking for all the world like lines drawn in blood. But the canyon was deserted, as empty of life as if none had ever been there. He wanted to lay there, to watch, to insist that something move, as if he were daring the earth to prove to him that he was not alone on its surface.

Finally, he saw the darting skitter of a ground squirrel and he felt a slight smile loosen the tightness in his jaw. Instinctively, he looked up at the sky, smeared with purple now as the few huge clouds darkened with the beginning of twilight. As if drawn by a magnet, his eye picked out the stately glide of a hawk, its broad wings motionless on the warm air rising from the heated wasteland. He watched the great predator circle once, then effortlessly change course, suddenly tucking its wings in and falling like a stone.

Fifty feet off the ground, directly across the canyon, the huge wings fanned out, the hawk braking in its plummet. Talons extended, it seemed almost to crash into the rocks, its wings beating furiously. He strained to hear the fluttering, but it was too far away. Then, abruptly, the hawk began to climb, the frenzied beating of its wings transformed now to deep, powerful strokes.

Lex saw the hawk's prey for the first time now, a lizard of some sort, its long tail rigid in its terror, the legs churning furiously as if the reptile thought it could run on the air. Thirty feet, then fifty, then higher, the hawk continued its climb. Lex shook his head in a mixture of wonder at the bird's strength and dismay at the lizard's fate.

He saw the beating wings lose their rhythm before he heard the gunshot, a distant crack that seemed so feeble at first he doubted that he had really heard it. The hawk continued to struggle, either losing its grip on the lizard or jettisoning the weight in order to climb faster. But it was useless. Lex watched the lizard fall among the rocks and disappear and the hawk begin to slide sidewise, one wing no longer equal to its task.

Mesmerized by the bird's distress, he lay there, knowing that he ought to move, knowing that whoever shot the bird was close by and that, whoever it was, he more than likely was one of Barton Rawlings's men. Only when the hawk fell below the rimrock, its wing still fluttering uselessly as it bounced once off the canyon wall then fell like a stone onto the tracks below, was Lex able to overcome the inertia that had pinned him to the ledge.

Scrambling backward, he groped for the Winchester, pulled it close, and then rolled into a niche between two boulders. As near as he could tell, the shot had come from the rim on his side. So, I'm not alone after all, he thought. And if there's somebody on this side, there just might be somebody on the far rim, as well. Moving cautiously, he crawled away from his cover, heading toward another boulder. He was breathing in short, sharp gasps, as if he'd just surfaced from a long way underwater. He glanced involuntarily at the sun, trying to gauge how much sunlight he had left. A half hour, at the most, he guessed.

Reaching cover again, he lay still, straining his

ears, hoping to tell whether it was a solitary gunman who had killed the hawk. As he lay there, he could feel the hammering of his heart. His blood beat in his ears, and his lips felt dry. His hands were sweaty as he thought how close he had come to walking right under the muzzle of the gunman.

He was about to move to the next cluster of rocks when he heard the dull clink of metal on stone. Then a hat brim appeared not fifty yards ahead, seeming almost to be floating just above the top of a large, flat rock. He watched the hat move, caught a glimpse of a face as the gunman stepped over something for a moment then sank out of sight.

While he waited for another glimpse, he debated whether to stay where he was or to move in and try to take the gunman prisoner. But even as he considered his options he realized how few they were, and how small the payoff was, no matter what he decided. Catching the man, if he was alone, might give him the chance to learn something he didn't already know. And if the gunman was not alone, the attempt might get him killed at worst and, at best, alert Rawlings and the others that their presence was known. But he crept closer all the same.

The gunman walked out to the edge then, as carelessly as if he believed he were alone on the canyon rim. He stood there with a rifle dangling from his right hand, staring down into the canyon as if to locate the fallen hawk. While Lex waited, the man rolled a cigarette, lit it, and flicked the match out over the edge where it fell out of sight, trailing a thin stream of gray smoke behind it.

Lex counted the seconds while the man sucked on

his cigarette. He was conscious of the light beginning to fade, knowing that in the dark, his task would be all the more difficult, assuming he could find the man at all once the sun went down. And not knowing where he was, in the dark, his movement would be severely limited. He closed the gap by another ten yards. He wasn't sure how close he was now, but he was close enough to hear the man exhale smoke.

Just as he was about to make a move, the gunman turned and flipped the cigarette butt over his shoulder into the canyon. "Paddy, you ever see a shot that good?" he asked. "Bang! Just like that. Plugged that bastard clean, dead center."

"Don't be breakin' your arm pattin' yourself on the back, Jimbo," another man, presumably the unseen Paddy, answered. "Anybody can get lucky once in a while."

"Lucky my ass. That was marksmanship. You couldn't do that in a million years."

"I don't have to, Jimbo. There's no money in it anyhow. You can shoot all the goddamned birds you want and it won't put a dime in your pocket."

"Come this time tomorrow, I'll have all the dimes I want in my pocket." Jimbo laughed. "So will you."

"You trust Rawlings, do you?" Paddy appeared suddenly, as if materializing out of thin air.

"Not much."

"Then what makes you think he'll give us a fair share?"

Jimbo grinned. Hefting the Springfield and patting its stock, he said, "I got a gun."

"So does Rawlings."

"I ain't scared of him. He's big, but that just means he'll make more noise when he falls."

"What makes you think he's gonna fall?"

Jimbo laughed. "That's easy. I'm gonna give him a little shove."

Paddy raked a fistful of fingers across his stubbled chin. "I'd be careful, I was you, Jimbo. Talkin' like that can get you kilt."

"Not likely. It's only us two up here."

"Radcliff and Billy are across the way."

"They can't hear nothing we say. 'Sides, Radcliff feels the same as I do. He don't trust Rawlings no more'n I do."

"Look, Jimbo, there's a dozen of us, counting Radcliff and me and you. How many of the twelve you think will back your play, if you go against Rawlings? Half of them are in his pocket to begin with, especially that snake-eyed little bastard brother of his. I wouldn't turn my back on that sumbitch with a dollar on the line, let alone a whole damn payroll. I figure we'll be lucky we get out of this mess alive. I'm starting to wish I'd never thrown in with Rawlings in the first place."

"Too late for that now, Paddy. Way too late for that. But if you stick with me, I think maybe we can fill our pockets some and walk away a whole lot richer than Mister Barton Rawlings intends for us to be. I know we can count on Radcliff. Maybe Billy, too. Radcliff is gonna find out tonight."

"What's he gonna do, ask him does he want to stick his neck in front of a buzz saw? Might as well, you run afoul of Rawlings."

"Course not. Radcliff is a whole lot smarter than

that, Paddy. There's ways of finding out what's on a man's mind without comin' out and askin' him. Hell, half the time a man don't know what he thinks until he starts talkin', then things sort of creep up on him, things he ain't never thought about before. He finds out what he thinks the same time he opens his mouth.''

Lex was creeping closer while the men talked. Every yard cost him, but he had to get closer. He wasn't sure how close was close enough, or what he was going to do once he managed, but he knew he had to think of something.

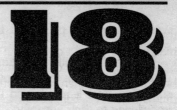

LEX LAY there quietly, watching the last few minutes of sunlight soak into the earth. When it was dark, he got to his knees and stared into the gloom, trying to re-create in his mind the terrain between him and the last place he'd seen Jimbo. The two men had stopped talking, and there was no way Lex could be certain that they hadn't moved. As near as he could tell from the conversation he'd overheard, they were going to spend the night on the rimrock.

He knew, too, from the same conversation, that two more men, identified only as Radcliff and Billy, were in a similar position across the canyon. The darkness protected him from discovery by those men, but if he were to make a move on Jimbo and Paddy, it would have to be silent. The use of a gun was out of the question. A single gunshot was all it would take to make his presence known, and even though Rawlings's men wouldn't know that he had several men with him, they would assume the worst. Rawlings would change his plans and Lex would be back to square one.

For nearly a half hour, Lex debated whether to make his way back to the canyon floor, tell Lute Olson what he'd learned, and try to turn that paltry knowledge to their advantage. If he stayed where he was, the sun would come up and he would have lost whatever edge he'd gained. On the other hand, if he tried to take Jimbo and Paddy and failed, he would be throwing away the slight edge his presence on the rimrock gave him, whatever the hell it was worth, for no gain. The margins were so close, he felt paralyzed. It seemed almost as if there were nothing he could do—except wait.

The silence was so complete, he was beginning to wonder whether the two men had gone to sleep for the night. Not a single word had drifted toward him through the darkness. He hadn't heard so much as the click of one pebble on another. For all the good his discovery had done, he might as well have been alone in the middle of the continent, a thousand miles from the nearest man. It made no difference that just a hundred and thirty feet below him lay the tentacles of progress, tentacles that were slowly going to strangle the wilderness, choke the life out of it and render it, if not hospitable, then at least harmless. That would take a while, of course, but it was a certainty. But when it finally happened, Lex knew that he would be obsolete. And for the moment, it seemed all he could do was sit there in the darkness and wait for it to happen.

It was more than an hour since the sun had gone down now. He had looked at his watch in the last subdued twilight, and it had been just short of nine o'clock. As nearly as he could guess, it should be somewhere between ten and ten-thirty.

"Billy? You there?"

The voice came out of nowhere, deep and resonant, and echoed back from the canyon off to the left as if it had fallen in on its way across. There was no answer.

"Billy?"

Once more, the echoes rattled around among the stones, bouncing off the walls of the canyon. Once more, there was no answer.

Lex strained to see if he could spot Jimbo, whose voice it was. He heard the rasp of a match, and suddenly saw Jimbo's bulky form outlined by the glow. Jimbo leaned forward, curled around the flickering flame for a moment, until his cigarette was lit, then faded back into the night.

"Sumbitch prob'ly ain't even up there yet," Jimbo muttered.

"That's right, Jimbo. Billy's got some smarts, unlike some I could mention," Paddy said, then laughed.

Lex could see the unblinking eye of Jimbo's cigarette. The big man took a deep drag, and the red aura seemed to swell until it edged the cowboy in ruby for a moment, then died away.

"He's probably sleeping, back at the camp. It's only you and me dumb enough to spend the night up here, Jimbo," Paddy said. "Makes me wish I was someplace else."

"You was back in camp, you'd have to sleep with

one eye open, Paddy," Jimbo said. "I'd want to make sure I woke up in the morning."

"What are you talkin' about?"

"You don't think Rawlings needs all of us, do you?"

"What's the difference. The more men, the easier to knock over the train."

"And the more cuts you got to make with the payroll. Once them rocks block the canyon, that train ain't goin' nowhere. And as soon as the crew gets the idea that unless they hand over the money, the other end of the canyon'll be blocked off, they'll fork it over right quick. How many men you think it takes to make them understand that?"

"Won't be as easy as you think, Jimbo. How in the hell are we gonna set off the second charge, anyhow? It's pretty near halfway up the canyon wall."

Jimbo laughed. "That's easy. You're goin' down on a rope. You gonna hang there like a goddamned spider with a match in your hand until the money's dumped out and the train backs out of the canyon."

"How come nobody told me?"

"I just did."

"I mean before now? I don't want to hang from no rope. I ain't gonna do it."

"You'll do it, all right. You'll do it, or Rawlings'll put a bullet through your head. You can bank on it."

"Naw. You do it, Jimbo. I don't wanna."

"And who the hell's gonna hold the rope? You? Hell's bells, Paddy, I weigh twice what you do, or damn near. That's the whole idea." He sucked on the cigarette again, and his face seemed to glow as if with some inner light for a split second, a bloody oval hanging in black space, back near the rim, as if it had just floated up from the canyon floor.

"I don't like heights."

"Don't matter what you like, Paddy. You want that money as much as I do. And you'll go on down the goddamned wall like Little Miss Muffet was waiting for you at the bottom." Again the cigarette bathed Jimbo in its red glow, then darted away like a firefly. "Billy, damn you, you there?"

Again there was no answer. Jimbo cursed in annoyance, flicked the cigarette high into the air where it flared as it arced overhead then fell into the black abyss. "Might as well get some sleep, Paddy," Jimbo said. "It's gonna be a long night."

Lex heard the big man's footsteps on the hard rock of the rim, then a grunt as he apparently lowered himself to the ground. Lex counted the minutes, waiting for another sound, some hint that Jimbo or Paddy might still be awake. But by midnight, he knew both men had gone to sleep. The more he thought about it, the more convinced he became that Paddy was a weak link. His reluctance to go along with his part in the plan, the mistrust that he shared with Jimbo, and the cynical truth Jimbo had articulated all suggested that, if he could be captured, he could be turned.

But how to get to him? Especially without waking Jimbo . . . that was the problem he had to solve. Despite the fact that Billy hadn't answered Jimbo's shouted hello, there was the distinct possibility that he and Radcliff were somewhere in the dark on the far side of the canyon. Whatever Lex decided to do, he was going to have to act as if they were. That meant silence, if not total, then as near as he could manage.

The Bowie knife on his belt was the only alternative, not a weapon he liked. The ugly blade always reminded him of a sidewinder. Once set loose, it didn't care who it bit. And Jimbo had a few inches and probably thirty pounds or so on him.

Loosening the knife in its sheath, he checked his revolver, made sure the cylinder was free and cracked it to check whether it was fully loaded. For a moment, he thought about leaving the Winchester behind, but realized that if the choice was using it or getting himself killed, he was going to shoot. Besides, in a pinch, the rifle could be used as a club, crude but effective.

Taking a deep breath, he got to his feet and started forward, placing each foot carefully in the darkness. There was some ambient light, but the ground was covered with slabs of rock, broken hunks of which lay hidden in the deep shadows cast by the larger stones. Footing was anything but certain, and running was absolutely out of the question. He would turn an ankle, if he didn't break one, within ten yards. And that was if he had luck on his side.

As he drew closer and closer, he could hear the heavy breathing of both sleeping men. One of them snored while the other seemed to be muttering to himself. He wished for a moment that he had the stealthy skill of an Apache.

Lex reached the large slab of red stone beyond which he knew Jimbo and Paddy had bedded down. Rather than go around it, he chose to go over the top. Clutching the Winchester in his left hand, he hauled himself up over the ragged face of the huge stone, rolled onto its top, and reached the far edge, where he lay still, listening. Paddy, his brogue even more pronounced in his sleep, was still muttering. Jimbo snorted like a bull, the sudden, sharp intake followed by a shuddering exhale loud enough to make the ground tremble.

Removing his hat, Lex peered over the edge into the black pool below him. He could just make out two mounds which he took to be the sleeping men. Getting to his feet then dropping quickly into a crouch, he yanked the Bowie knife from its sheath. Taking a deep breath, he jumped. For all he knew, he might have been jumping into the canyon itself, it was so dark below.

The impact rattled his teeth. It wasn't possible to steel himself because he couldn't see the ground, and when it finally came, it caught him unprepared. He grunted, and heard Jimbo stirring immediately.

Spinning, he leaped onto the still groggy man, pressed the knife to Jimbo's throat, and hissed, "You make one sound, and so help me, I'll kill you."

Jimbo nodded his head slightly to indicate that he understood. His breath stank as he exhaled into Lex's face.

"Now," Lex whispered, "I'm going to get up, and you're going to get on your hands and knees, understand?"

Jimbo nodded.

"Then you're going to crawl over to your partner and wake him up. Got it?"

Jimbo nodded again. "All right, then, easy now . . ."

Lex was in a crouch, the edge of the knife still

resting on Jimbo's windpipe. He had to pull it away a couple of inches to let the bigger man move. Like some strange beast out of mythology, they crept toward the sleeping Paddy, Lex resting a hand on Jimbo's back to keep track of him, and to feel for any tightening of the muscles that might indicate a sudden move.

When they reached Paddy's bedroll, Lex leaned close enough to whisper in Jimbo's ear. "Put a hand over his mouth when you wake him up. I don't want any shouting, understand?"

Jimbo nodded his head that he understood. He leaned forward, and Lex heard Paddy's regular breathing interrupted by the clasped hand. Then he heard something else, the click of metal, and he realized almost too late that it was a revolver being cocked. He threw himself onto Jimbo's back just as the big man turned. Outlined against the sky, Lex could see the shape of a pistol in Jimbo's left hand.

Off balance, he fell heavily and Jimbo grunted as he tried to get to his feet. Lex kicked out, caught him behind the right knee, and Jimbo went down. Lex twisted, bringing the Bowie knife around, its butt jammed against the rocks. Then Jimbo moaned as he landed on Lex's outstretched arm.

Jimbo inhaled sharply, and his breath gurgled in his lungs as he tried to twist away. Lex held on to the knife for all he was worth as one of Jimbo's huge hands closed over his curled fingers. The knife was buried to the hilt in Jimbo's chest, and he was breathing oddly, little, explosive inhalations, each one accompanied by a high-pitched moan of pain and followed by the rumbling gurgle of blood in the pierced lung.

Reaching back with his free hand, Lex closed it on a large rock, brought it up high overhead and cracked it sharply down on Jimbo's skull. The big man lay still, his breath shallow and ragged now.

Lex was about to get to his feet when he felt the pressure of something cold against the back of his neck.

He didn't need to be told what it was. Then Paddy whispered, "You better have a real good story, mister, or I'm gonna paint these rocks with your brains."

LEX FELT the gun pull away from his head. He sat there panting, knowing that some-one, almost certainly Paddy, was standing just a couple of feet away. But since the muzzle of the .45 revolver was between them, and Paddy had his finger curled around the trigger, it might as well have been a mile.

The silence was broken only by the gurgle of Jimbo's breathing, which seemed to be growing fainter and less regular with almost every inhalation.

After a couple of minutes, Lex said, "You'd better see to your friend. He's hurt bad."

"He's no friend of mine, cowboy."

"Glad I don't ride with you," Lex said.

"Shut up!" There was a petulant edge to the command, as if Paddy's feelings had been hurt by the remark. "Just keep your mouth shut. I got to think."

Lex heard the shuffle of feet on the stone, and sensed that Paddy was backing away a bit. The Ranger turned to look over his shoulder, but Paddy wasn't much more than a gray shade against the black sky.

"No need for this, you know," Lex said. "You haven't done anything wrong, yet."

"I told you to shut your mouth, and I meant it. I ain't gonna tell you again. Less'n I ask you a question, you don't say a goddamned word, understand?"

Lex shook his head, knowing that Paddy couldn't see it.

"I asked you if you understood me, cowboy. If you don't, maybe I'd best put a bullet in you right now. Then it won't matter none."

"Don't be a fool, Paddy."

"How'd you know my name?"

"We all know your name, Paddy. Don't you know that?"

"All? Who's all? There ain't nobody else with you, or they woulda done something to help you by now."

"Maybe, and maybe not. You haven't done much for Jimbo, there, have you?"

"That's different. He's prob'ly dead already, whether he keeps breathin' for a few minutes or not. No way he's gonna last."

"That's probably true. But there's no need for anybody else to get hurt."

"You don't hear too good, do you. I want you to shut up, so I can think."

"Whatever you say, Paddy. We have all night."

"Stop that. Stop sayin' we. You're all by your lonesome. I know that. You're just tryin' to rattle me some. But it won't work. I don't rattle easy."

"Seems to me you're already rattled, Paddy. And you know what? You got a right to be. You're in a very deep hole, Paddy. And right now, there's no-body to throw you a rope. You think goin' down the wall to that dynamite was gonna be fun, wait till you try to climb out of this one. I wouldn't want to be in your shoes for all the tea in China."

"I told you, I don't rattle easy."

"Maybe you should try calling your friends Billy and Radcliff again. Of course, they won't answer. And you know why?"

"Why?"

"Because Sheriff Olson—you know him, don't you—from Monroe? Anyhow, he's across the way. Billy and Radcliff are already in handcuffs, so even if they answer you, they can't help you none. Course, they're lucky. Rawlings would have put a bullet in their backs the first chance he got, anyhow. That much I know. And I think you know that, too. Don't you, Paddy? You know that."

"That's bullshit. You sound just like Jimbo, and look where it got him."

"I grant you, it ain't an easy thing to lie there and bleed to death, drowning in your own damn blood, Paddy. No sir, that ain't an easy thing. But the fact is, dead is dead. It don't matter whether it's slow, like Jimbo there, or fast, like it was gonna be for you and Jimbo and Billy and Radcliff, and. . . ."

"Shut up, damn it!"

"All right, I won't say anything else. But what I am gonna do is I'm gonna get up and take a look at Jimbo, see if he's past saving or not. I'd hate to think we could have done something for him while we just sat here jawin' at one another. That'd be a hard thing, don't you think, to spend the rest of your life knowing you let a friend die when you could have saved him? I know I wouldn't want to live with something like that."

Lex got to his feet slowly. He could just make out Paddy when he turned to look over his shoulder, but there was no doubt the gun in Paddy's hand was still leveled at him.

Lex groped toward the sound of Jimbo's ragged breathing, dropped to one knee and bent to listen to the wounded man's chest. It sounded as if one lung were still in working order, as if the knife, which Lex couldn't find, had punctured only one. But the width of the blade would have done a lot of damage, and Jimbo had landed hard, driving it all the way in. More than likely, a couple of arteries had been severed.

Lex felt for a pulse, but it was faint and irregular. He looked in Paddy's direction. "He won't last much longer, Paddy. I guess it'll be a little easier, not having to listen to that damn gurgling sound, huh? Once that train comes through, I reckon you can just ride away, with your pockets jingling. If Rawlings lets you, that is."

"He'll let me. Don't you worry none about that."

"The buzzards'll take care of Jimbo. You won't even have to bury him."

"You still didn't tell me who you are," Paddy said. "I think maybe it's about time you start answering a few questions."

"What difference does it make who I am? You have all the answers, anyhow, to hear you tell it. You know everything you want to know about Barton Rawlings. You know about the railroad payroll. You know all about Schuster, Crandall and Keats. What more do you need to know?"

"Who the fuck are you? That's one thing I need to know, and by God you're gonna tell me, or I'm gonna use this gun. Then it won't matter who you are. Will it?"

"If you say so."

"All right. The name's Cranshaw. Lex Cranshaw."

"You a lawman? You must be or there ain't no reason for you to be here. So, I guess that sort of answers itself, don't it? What are you, a marshal? A sheriff, something like that?"

"Something like that," Lex said. "You mind if I smoke?"

"Suit yourself. It'll give me time to figure out what to do with you."

Lex thanked him, reached into his pocket for the fixings, and rolled a cigarette. Returning the pouch to his pocket, he licked the paper, then thumbed a match into flame and lit the cigarette. Exhaling the first long drag, he watched the smoke drift away on the breeze before saying, "You know, Paddy, if you were to throw in with me now, I can guarantee you won't go to prison."

"I can guarantee that my own self, Mister Cranshaw. I got a gun, remember?"

"Yeah, you got a gun, but guns aren't everything. There's a difference between me and Barton Rawlings."

"Oh yeah, what's that?"

"You can trust me . . ."

"You're starting to sound like Jimbo."

"Jimbo was right. I know more about Rawlings than you do. A lot more. And one thing I can tell you for sure. He likes to kill people. And if killing somebody puts a little more money in his pocket, so much the better. Not that he needs an excuse. He's nothing but a two-bit bully anyhow."

"Listen, Mister Cranshaw, come tomorrow morning, after that train comes through, I'm gonna climb onto my horse and ride away. I'll never see Barton Rawlings again as long as I live. But I'll have four or five thousand dollars to stake me to whatever I want to do."

"You really think Rawlings will let you climb on that horse, do you, Paddy?"

"Sure I do."

"Well, if he does, it'll just be so he can shoot you in the back before you get ten yards."

"I don't believe that."

"It doesn't much matter what you believe if I'm right, does it, Paddy?"

"I think maybe you should be quiet now, Cranshaw. You're making me nervous. I don't want to shoot you until I'm ready, but if you keep jabberin', my finger's likely to get a mite itchy, if you know what I mean."

Lex lapsed into silence. Paddy was a tougher nut to crack than he'd thought. The man seemed singleminded, as if his cut of the payroll robbery was the only thing that mattered, and whatever he had to do to get it, he was determined to do.

"You know," Lex finally said, when he'd puffed on the cigarette for the last time and flicked it down into the canyon, "there's a reward on Rawlings's head. It isn't much, but it's honest pay."

"How much?"

"Fifteen hundred dollars, maybe two thousand. I don't know the exact amount, because half a dozen banks have put up a piece. You know he'd killed several men before Schuster, don't you. I mean, it's not like he killed Schuster in a fit of anger and doesn't have any choice now. He's killed before with a lot less provocation, so you shouldn't be thinking he's just some poor slob who got backed into a corner."

"It don't . . . what the hell's that?" Paddy took a step forward, then another. "Look," he said. Lex could just make out the pointing arm, and turned to see what Paddy was calling to his attention.

Two hundred yards away, the rimrock was clearly outlined by an orange glow from somewhere down in the canyon. Across the way, Lex could see the far wall, shadows stabbing up into the night from outcrops of rock and the few hardy plants that clung to the sheer face. Gray smoke in thin tendrils drifted up into the darkness above the rim.

The light was moving, coming closer.

"Must be the train," Paddy said. "It's early."

Lex shook his head and got to his feet. "You'd hear the train, and you'd see plenty of black smoke."

"What is it, then?"

"Let's take a look."

"You stay right where you are. I'll look. Don't you even move, because I'll shoot you if I hear a sound, understand?"

Paddy moved past him then, and walked to the edge. He lay down on the ground and leaned out over the rim to peer as far through the twisting canyon as he could see.

"I'm coming over there," Lex said. When Paddy didn't answer, he walked toward the rim and lay down beside the Irishman.

Just coming into view were three men. One held a torch overhead, its orange flames flickering and filling the deep ravine with dancing light. And one of the men was Barton Rawlings.

"Train must be coming," Paddy said.

"Why don't you wait and see what happens, Paddy," Lex suggested.

"What do you mean?"

"Just wait, that's all."

Paddy didn't answer, but he didn't call attention to himself, either. They watched as Rawlings took the torch and the other two stopped a few yards to the right.

"Hold it higher, Bart," one of them said. "It's right here somewhere." By their clothing, Lex recognized the two men he'd seen planting the dynamite earlier that afternoon.

"Hurry up, damn it," Rawlings barked.

"Here it is." Lex watched as the man planted his back against the wall and made a stirrup of his hands. He boosted the second, smaller man, as Rawlings backed away a bit. With the torch below and behind him, the small man's face was obscured by shadow for a moment, then a match flared, and Lex recognized Martin Rawlings.

The fuse on the dynamite suddenly spluttered, showering sparks as it burned, and Martin pushed out away from the wall in preparation for dismounting.

At first, Lex wasn't sure what had happened. But when Paddy said, "Jesus Christ!" it was clear that something had. The second gunshot was unmistakable. Then Barton Rawlings started to run, leaving the torch on the ground behind him.

The ground shook, and Lex instinctively hugged the ledge. Dust boiled up from the canyon, backlit by the guttering torch on the ground, and it looked like an orange haze was welling up out of a hole in the earth.

"Christ, did you see that?" Paddy asked.

"Did you?" Lex answered.

"Sumbitch shot his own brother and left him there. He might be buried alive . . ."

"Not for long," Lex said.

I T TOOK them a long time to get down in the dark. Paddy had wanted to bring his horse and just ride away, but Lex had convinced him that he might just as well stay and help. At least he would have the reward to show for his efforts. It might not match his share of the payroll, but it was honest money. Even that hadn't done the trick. The clincher was Lex pointing out that, if he helped bring Rawlings down, Paddy wouldn't have to spend the rest of his life looking over his shoulder, wondering when the big man would finally catch up to him.

Now, they were ready.

"We can't go through the canyon," Lex said, "so we'll have to go around. Paddy will lead us to Rawlings's camp."

"You trust the little potato eater, do you, Lex?" Olson wanted to know.

Mike O'Hara took exception to the categorization, but Olson glared at him and he shut up.

"Yeah, I do, Sheriff. I trust him."

"Why?"

"Because I saw the look on his face when Rawlings killed those two men. If you'd seen it, you'd trust him, too. I guarantee you."

"We'll still have to keep an eye on him."

"Fine. As long as he leads us to the camp, I'm satisfied. But I did promise him the reward money, whatever it might be."

"Don't seem fair, really. All these boys puttin' their necks on the line and that little bastard getting all the reward money."

"A deal's a deal, Lute. You know that. And you'd have done the same in my shoes."

Olson nodded. "Yeah, I would have. But I wouldn't have liked it much then, neither."

"The problem will be the two men up top," Lex said. "They didn't answer Jimbo when he called, but that doesn't mean they weren't up there. And we don't want to be in a position where they can fire on us from high ground like that."

"We can't do much about it till daylight, Lex. What do you figure we ought to do?"

"Maybe leave three men here, tell them to head up there as soon as they can see well enough to make the climb."

"I'll stay," Childress volunteered. "No need for either one of you to stay. You know more about gunslingin' than I do anyhow."

"Thanks, Roy," Lex said. "But you be careful. Don't move until you got daylight enough to get up top there in a hurry. The two men might not even be there, but if they are, don't take any chances."

"No, sir, I won't. I'll keep Jace and Dexter with me, if it's all right."

Dexter laughed. "Long as you don't shoot nobody but bad guys, Roy, I don't mind stayin'."

"Me neither," Jace said. "Just so's the sheriff leaves some bandages behind, in case Roy wants to hit hisself in the nose with a rock."

"You boys take it easy on Roy," Olson said. "He's all right."

"Sure he is," Jace said, "long as you keep an eye on him. But we'll do that, Sheriff."

"That cuts us down pretty thin, Cranshaw," Olson said, turning to the Ranger.

"I know it, Lute. But we have surprise on our side. It'll help some."

"Enough, I hope."

"We'd better go. You ready, Paddy?"

Paddy nodded. "Yes, sir, I am."

"Once we get there, you just duck out of the way. No need for you to get involved in any gunplay."

Paddy sucked on a tooth before answering. "Seems like to me I maybe ought to. Rawlings's got it coming, and I'll be happy to be there. I know you want him alive, but I don't much care whether he takes one in the head."

"That's enough jawin', boys," Olson barked. "Let's mount up."

"Okay, Paddy," Lex said, "you lead the way. You can ride one of the spare horses."

Paddy climbed into the saddle, taking the reins from Roy's hand. "Thank you," he said. "I'll take good care of your mount."

It took nearly two hours to circle through the rugged country, and by the time they dismounted, the last handful of stars was already beginning to disappear. The sky was a sheet of dark gray, and the eastern horizon had a hint of pale gray marking the boundary between earth and sky.

Paddy held up a hand, and leaned closer to Lex, almost as if he feared being overheard. "It's pretty much a straight shot from here, Mister Cranshaw, but we'd best be careful the last bit. The terrain is pretty flat, and if anybody's up, he'll spot us a long way off. There's a creek and a stand of cottonwoods, and as soon as the tops of them trees come over the horizon we better get down and walk."

Lex nodded, then fell back to let Sheriff Olson know what they had to do. Olson stood in the stirrups and turned to pass the word. "You men keep them horses quiet. I don't want to hear nothing so much as a jingle, not even two pennies in your pocket, if you got that much, understand? And limber up your knee joints, we're gonna go in shank's mare, pretty soon."

The men grumbled, but quickly fell silent when Olson barked, "Quiet, I told you, damn it!"

They rode another mile. In the graying dawn, the crowns of a cottonwood stand floated ahead of them like islands of coal on a gray sea. "That's it," Paddy said, stabbing a finger toward the treetops.

"All right, men, pull up," Lex said.

He looked at Olson, who nodded. "You're the boss, Cranshaw. Tell us what you want us to do."

Lex dismounted. "We'll go on foot from here. Once we get close enough to see how things lie, we'll make our next decision. I want everybody to be as quiet as if his life depended on it, because it just might." Turning to O'Hara, he added, "Mike, you stay here with the horses."

The surveyor started to protest, but Lex stopped him with a raised hand. "Somebody's got to do it. It might as well be you."

"Just remember I got three months' pay riding on you boys." O'Hara grinned. "I'd be grateful if you'd save that much, at least." The men laughed uneasily. It was starting to dawn on them that in less than an hour they might be shooting to kill . . . and that other men might be shooting to kill them, too.

They went in single file, Lex at the point, Olson a step behind and to the right. Olson wanted to talk, but it was clear that Lex was in no mood for idle chatter, and the injunction to silence permitted no exceptions, especially not the jabbering of a nervous old man.

They were able to get within three hundred yards of the campsite. The sun still hadn't started to dye the sky its morning red, but it was easy enough to pick out the shapes of the picketed horses under the cottonwoods. Using binoculars, Lex scanned the camp, counting bodies, or at least lumps he took for bodies. There were fewer than he expected.

Pulling Paddy aside, he asked, "How many men did Rawlings have altogether?"

"There was twelve, counting him. Why?"

"I count only six. Subtracting you and Jimbo and the two men he buried under the rockfall should leave eight. Where are the other two?"

"Must be Billy and Radcliff are up top the canyon, like they was supposed to be."

"I hope so," Lex muttered. "I don't want any surprises."

The railroad tracks lay between Lex and the silent

camp. Apparently, Rawlings was leaving nothing to
chance. The canyon was already blocked, he was
sleeping within earshot of the passing train, and he
had positioned two snipers above the blockade, just
to be sure. He had covered all the bases. All except
one—he hadn't counted on Lex Cranshaw.

Pointing out the sleeping men and passing the
glasses down the line, Lex tallied the odds. He had six
men and so did Rawlings. Rawlings and his men were
sleeping, which gave Lex the advantage of surprise,
but Rawlings and his men had nothing to lose, and
Rawlings himself was a hardened killer, so the pendu-
lum swung back the other way. Whatever happened,
Lex was determined to get Rawlings first, and the rest
would follow. The big man was the key, and if he was
yanked loose, the whole house of cards would probably collapse. Or so Lex hoped.

"Let's go," he said. "Spread out and I don't want
any shooting unless it's necessary. But if it is, shoot to
kill."

The men muttered nervously, as if the final command had forced them finally to confront the reality
they had been doing their best to ignore.

They were within a hundred and fifty yards when
Lex saw one of the sleeping forms move. He hissed a
command to halt, and the men froze in their tracks. A
moment later the man sat up. Lex could see clearly
enough to know it wasn't Rawlings. Crossing his fingers, he watched as the man stretched and hoped
that he wouldn't wake the others.

It seemed like he held his breath forever while the
man got to his feet, then tiptoed off into the bushes
down by the creekbank. Letting his breath out again,

Lex whispered, "All right, you saw him, you know where he is. Remember that and go ahead on."

They had just started to move again when the mournful wail of a train whistle sounded. One blast, then a second and a third. Like the call of some alien bird, it drifted toward them out of the early morning. It wasn't loud enough to wake the sleeping men. Not yet, but it didn't matter, because the man who'd already risen had heard it. Rushing out of the brush, still buttoning his trousers, he started to shout. "Wake up, you bastards, train's comin'."

A moment later, it looked as if someone had poked a stick into a hill of giant ants. The men scrambled quickly. Sleeping in their clothes, their boots already on, all they had to do was saddle their mounts. Once in the saddle, they would have an impossible advantage over the posse on foot.

"All right, men," Lex shouted, "let's go."

Without waiting to see whether they would respond, he raced ahead, crossing the tracks with a single leap. The bandits saw him coming and opened fire. All hell broke loose in a split second as gunshots exploded behind him and bullets whistled over his head from both directions. He turned to see that he was a good twenty yards ahead of the others, who seemed unable to run and shoot at the same time. Olson was waving his arms frantically to urge them on, but it seemed to have no effect.

Lex saw the largest of the men, a figure that could only be that of Barton Rawlings, a rifle in hand, come storming out of the cottonwood stand. The man had courage, Lex thought. I have to give him that much.

The gunfire had all but stopped now. Rawlings's

men were scurrying around, uncertain whether to mount up or follow their leader toward the attacking posse. Rawlings suddenly realized the lawmen had no horses, and he turned to his men. "Git in the saddle, you damn fools. They're on foot."

Lex dropped to one knee then and brought up his Winchester. Aiming quickly, he fired once, then again. Both shots hit their mark, and one of the horses went down. "Listen to me, you men," Lex shouted. "You want to walk all the way back to Wilson's Gap, you go ahead and mount up. I'll shoot every damn horse."

"Come on, what the hell are you waiting for," Rawlings yelled. "Mount up and git them!"

DURING THE long silence, Lex could hear the whistle of the approaching train once more. In the lightening gray, it sounded like a banshee, one long, echoing moan, as if a single lost soul were hurrying home ahead of the sun. He glanced behind him, and saw that Olson had managed to gather the posse, but they were still frozen in the same motionless confusion that had gripped Rawlings and his men.

"Give it up, Rawlings," Lex yelled. "There's no way you can escape. And you can't take the train. There's extra security on board. It's over."

"Go to hell, Cranshaw," the big man answered. "I ain't gonna spend the rest of my life in prison. And I sure as hell ain't gonna stretch a rope, not for no-body!"

He fired once, then wheeled and broke for the trees.

"Stop!" Lex shouted. But Rawlings ignored him, plunging through the scattered bedrolls and toward the nearest horse. One of his men stood there, the reins in his fist and when Rawlings tried to tug them free, the man resisted. Lex could see it coming, and shouted, but before the words were out of his mouth, the report of the gunshot echoed off the trees.

With a jerk of his arm, Rawlings had the reins free then slammed his pistol barrel into the man's face. Even at his distance, Lex could hear the crunch of bone. The man fell to his knees and Rawlings shot him again, this time in the face at point-blank range.

He vaulted into the saddle then, with surprising grace for so big a man, and he was in full gallop even as Lex started to run. For a moment Lex forgot he was charging headlong into a half dozen of the men he'd come to arrest, but when it dawned on him, it also dawned that he didn't care.

The men were stock-still, jaws agape, stunned into statuary after the brutal scene they had just witnessed. Lex reached a horse and the owner offered no resistance when he snatched the reins and swung aboard. Rawlings was already a hundred yards ahead of him, but Lex paused long enough to shout, "You men throw down your guns." Without waiting to see whether they complied, he dug his spurs into the borrowed horse's flanks. As the animal exploded into motion, Lex heard the clatter of weapons on the ground, and allowed himself a grim smile. That much, at least, was taken care of.

Once clear of the cottonwoods, Rawlings crossed the creek and headed straight for the canyon, a little more than a mile away. Neither man was familiar with his mount, and that would slow them both, but Lex figured Rawlings's size advantage was a liability now.

He was closing, but more slowly than he wanted. Expecting Rawlings to veer off to the side rather than try to scale the slopes and go over the top of the butte, he waited for the outlaw to make a move. It wouldn't make sense to try the canyon. Rawlings knew it had been blocked by the rockfall, and there was no point in having to give up his horse.

But Rawlings continued dead on for the canyon. When he reached its mouth, he jerked the horse into a skidding stop and leaped from the saddle, yanking a rifle from the saddle boot, and sprinting for the base of the steep slope.

Leaping from boulder to boulder, Rawlings zig-zagged the first twenty-five yards uphill, then turned and fired, just as Lex was dismounting. The bullet went wide, struck the horse in the head, and it fell like a poleaxed steer, a single whimper and shuddering exhale its only sounds.

Lex thought the shot had been by accident until Rawlings turned the rifle on his own borrowed mount. Only then did he realize what Rawlings was doing. The outlaw was counting on getting to the top, where he could join up with the two men he'd posted there, get a horse, and leave Lex stranded on foot.

Lex shook his head in something akin to admiration. "Smart," he whispered. "Real smart."

The third shot was intended for Lex, and narrowly missed him as he managed to dive behind his fallen mount just as Rawlings brought the rifle to bear. The bullet thudded into the saddle not three inches above his head.

The chase up the slope was a home game for

Rawlings. He had the high ground, and he had plenty of cover. He also had the initiative, moving when he chose, and leaving Lex no choice but to react. Trying to charge ahead would be suicide.

Boulder by boulder, Rawlings worked his way up, sometimes moving no more than four or five feet, sometimes sprinting ten or fifteen yards at a clip. The arduous climb seemed to be slowing him, but just a little.

Lex hadn't bothered to call for Rawlings to surrender, because it was apparent Rawlings had no such intention. And Lex needed his wind for the uphill sprints.

The big man was not signaling his dashes from cover to cover with a gunshot to force Lex down, so all the Ranger could do was wait. And follow, getting to his feet and scrambling uphill each time he heard the thud of Rawlings's feet on the sandy ground.

When Rawlings finally reached the top he took cover behind a stone slab, and Lex, nearly forty yards behind, had to lay flat. He couldn't see Rawlings, and he heard nothing. He knew that Rawlings could be baiting a trap for him, or that he could have slipped away, leaving Lex to lie there, not sure whether to risk a headlong charge.

When five minutes had gone by, without a sound from the top of the butte, Lex decided he had no choice. Getting to his feet, he ducked into a crouch and darted into the clear, steeling himself for the slam of a bullet that might kill him before the sound of the gunshot reached his ears.

His knees ached, but he zigzagged from rock to rock. And nothing happened. Pausing to catch his breath, all he could hear was the pounding of his heart and the rasp of breath in his parched throat.

Covering the last ten yards in a single straight sprint, he dove on top of the slab behind which Rawlings had taken cover. Far ahead, he could just make out the big man, almost a quarter of a mile in the lead now. He knew he'd had no choice but to wait, but he couldn't shake the thought that Rawlings was laughing at him, and it made him mad, mad as hell.

Leaping off the flat slab, he plunged ahead, knowing that Rawlings probably had an insuperable lead. His only hope was that Childress and his men were up there somewhere, and that they would see Rawlings before he saw them.

He half expected to hear Rawlings call to Billy or Radcliff, but there was only the pounding of his feet on the broken ground to break the stillness.

Lex was closing the gap, but not fast enough. He was still three hundred yards behind when a gunshot shattered the silence. Lex stopped in his tracks and saw Rawlings spin, then charge back in his direction.

"Goddamn, Roy, you're there," Lex whispered. He wanted to shout it at the top of his lungs and would have if he hadn't been so winded.

Rawlings veered toward the rimrock now, and dashed straight toward him. He must have seen that he was outnumbered up ahead, and believed that Lex was the lesser obstacle.

Angling toward the rimrock, Lex took cover behind a large rock and waited. He didn't expect to take Rawlings by surprise, but he didn't want to stand in the open, either. By now, the big man would be desperate, and only when he saw that he had no chance at all of escape would he listen to reason.

Lex saw three figures zigzagging among the boulders a good two hundred yards behind Rawlings, who kept swiveling his head, looking for Lex and trying to monitor the pursuit.

When he was fifty yards away, Lex fired two quick shots into the air and stepped into the clear.

"That's it, Rawlings," he shouted. "It's over. Give it up, man!"

Rawlings froze, then started to laugh. He stood upright, the rifle dangling from one hand, the other pushing his hat back. The sun was poking above the horizon now, and sent a long shadow out ahead of Lex, almost like a black, accusatory finger pointing at Barton Rawlings.

Rawlings laughed loudly now, almost a bellow, that roared back at them both from the abyss beside them. Tilting his head a little, as if to glance at the sun, he spat in a long arc that caught the red sunlight and curved down into the canyon like a spurt of liquid rubies.

"Sumbitch, Cranshaw, you ain't as dumb as I thought."

"Put down your gun, Rawlings."

Rawlings shook his head. Glancing over his shoulder at the three men behind him for a moment, he took a deep breath. "Told you once, I ain't goin' to prison and I ain't gonna stretch a rope."

"Yeah, you are. One or the other."

Rawlings grinned at him. "Naw," he said. "I ain't."

Lex took a step toward him, then stopped in

stunned amazement as Rawlings took one step then leaped out over the rimrock, the big body once more displaying surprising grace as it curled in the air for a moment then plunged straight down. He never uttered a sound.

And Lex cringed in anticipation, waiting for the thud on the canyon floor. When it came, it was a dull and distant sound, barely loud enough to echo, and only once.

Then it was gone.

Dan Mason is the pseudonym of a full-time writer who lives in upstate New York with his family.

Saddle-up to these

THE REGULATOR *by Dale Colter*
Sam Slater, blood brother of the Apache
and a cunning bounty-hunter, is out to
collect the big price on the heads of the
murderous Pauley gang. He'll give them
a single choice: surrender and live, or go
for your sixgun.

THE REGULATOR—Diablo At Daybreak
by Dale Colter
The Governor wants the blood of the
Apache murderers who ravaged his
daughter. He gives Sam Slater a choice:
work for him, or face a noose. Now
Slater must hunt down the deadly rene-
gade Chacon…Slater's Apache brother.

THE JUDGE *by Hank Edwards*
Federal Judge Clay Torn is more than a
judge—sometimes he has to be the jury
and the executioner. Torn pits himself
against the most violent and ruthless
man in Kansas, a battle whose final ver-
dict will judge one man right…and one
man dead.

THE JUDGE—War Clouds
by Hank Edwards
Judge Clay Torn rides into Dakota where
the Cheyenne are painting for war and
the army is shining steel and loading
lead. If war breaks out, someone is
going to make a pile of money on a river
of blood.

VALLEY OF WILD HORSES
0-06-100221-6 $3.95

WILDERNESS TREK
0-06-100260-7 $3.99

THE VANISHING AMERICAN
0-06-100295-X $3.99

CAPTIVES OF THE DESERT
0-06-100292-5 $3.99

THE SPIRIT OF THE BORDER
0-06-100293-3 $3.99

BLACK MESA
0-06-100291-7 $3.99

ROBBERS' ROOST
0-06-100280-1 $3.99

UNDER THE TONTO RIM
0-06-100294-1 $3.99